Threesome

Also by Brenda L. Thomas

Fourplay: the dance of sensuality

The Velvet Rope

Four Degrees of Heat
(with Crystal Lacey Winslow,
Rochelle Alers & ReShonda Tate Billingsley)

Threesome

Where Seduction, Power & Basketball Collide

Brenda L. Thomas

POCKET BOOKS

New York   London   Toronto   Sydney

POCKET BOOKS, a division of Simon & Schuster, Inc.
1230 Avenue of the Americas, New York, NY 10020

ISBN-13: 978-0-7434-9705-3

ISBN-10: 0-7434-9705-8

First Pocket Books trade paperback edition May 2005

10   9   8   7   6   5   4   3   2   1

Manufactured in the United States of America

For information regarding special discounts for bulk purchases,
please contact Simon & Schuster Special Sales at 1-800-456-6798 or
business@simonandschuster.com

If ever there was an angel,
my sister Gwen Brown was one.

July 1947 to December 1996

ACKNOWLEDGMENTS

All Praises to Allah, Most Gracious, Most Merciful

I am blessed with more than just the ability to write. I am blessed to have known people to help me in this process of writing and publishing more than a book but a long-time dream. Throughout this process I have been overwhelmed by the love, prayers, support, phone calls, E-mails, and guidance I have received. I must though acknowledge those who specifically contributed.

I would ask that my blessings go to the following people: Kelisha Rawlinson, my daughter and manager who's been with me on this journey; Kelvin Rawlinson, my son, here's hoping you get your drop-top Benz; Horace Owens, my muse; Leigh and Bob.

Karsch, my friends and designer; my brothers, Joe, Gregory (who reminded me to hit my knees), and Jeffery Thomas; Tracy Diamond, who dusted off her editorial skills; Earl Cox, who helped me pull this off; Carmen

Rodriguez-Carrion, my publicist; Kim Gerald, my sister-friend who pushed me and gave tough love; Barbara Campbell, my niece who always thinks I forget about her; Denise Robinson, who talked to me at least three times a day over the phone; and Maurice Carter, my future son-in-law. Thanks to my nieces, nephews, cousins, aunts, uncles, and extended family, who spread the word, and my ancestors for building the foundation I now stand on.

And saving the best for last, I thank my parents, Mary and Thurmond Thomas, for reminding me to "Just be yourself, Bones." And endless love goes to my grand-daughters, Jazz, Briana, and Jada, the joys of my life.

If love were perfect, then it wouldn't be love.

PROLOGUE

SASHA
Philadelphia
May 1998

I thought I heard a noise downstairs, but figured it was just my imagination. No need to investigate—it was the same noise I always heard when I was here alone. Always thinking somebody might be sneaking into the house. I didn't have to worry tonight, though, because he was here with me. Maybe not for the whole night, but he would be here for a little while. His three, maybe four hours were usually enough to hold me over until the next time. And if someone did enter my home while he was here, then he'd be able to protect me, which is all I really wanted.

But there was the noise again. I lay there hoping it was the house settling, but I knew that this old house had long since settled. I turned to look at him; both of us had been unable to say anything since he'd come inside me. Sometimes it was like that. Our lovemaking was so strong, so intense, that it took our words away, leaving us unable to talk about it until the next day. As I looked at him, I was amazed to hear the creaking of the stairs. Someone was definitely in the house. Before I knew it, she appeared in my bedroom doorway.

PAULETTE

I knew they were together tonight. I'd followed him there myself instead of having my cousin do it. I knew the house because I'd slowly driven by it on numerous occasions once I had all the evidence. Tonight I watched him ring the bell instead of using his key. The lights were on downstairs, so I could make out through the slightly open blinds her greeting him with a kiss. Then I saw him sit at the kitchen table, and I sat motionless watching her shadow move about fixing his plate.

I'd always known he cheated, but I usually reasoned that all men did it, my husband being no exception. I knew he was busy. I mean, with two jobs and his various community activities, he was always gone. Things were still the same at home, though. The bills were paid and he treated us good, but at times he just seemed happy about something that I wasn't part of.

I mean, I had a busy life too, with my job, our son's activities, and all the things I was involved in at church. I was often tired and distracted. I knew our marriage wasn't perfect, but it was solid. We had a comfortable home and were part of a decent community. I prayed he would return to church but he continued to profess to being Muslim. I didn't argue because at least he believed in

God. My husband was always home for the holidays and each year he would agree to celebrate our wedding anniversary however I chose. But still I noticed.

Then our lovemaking changed. All of a sudden he didn't seem to mind when I didn't want to have sex and often I found myself having to initiate it. And why, I wondered, was he suggesting different things for dinner? Salads, fish, pasta, even dessert when it wasn't a holiday. All the time talking about being healthy, taking vitamins and going to the gym.

They were just little signs. Nothing obvious, like staying out all night. I mean, once in a while he would come home late, at three or four in the morning, but it wasn't a big deal. What confused me the most was the *unobvious.* Did he or did he not smell slightly different? It wasn't another woman's perfume, just the faint scent of another woman's aura surrounding him.

Then he purchased a pager, and for a while he had a cell phone. I knew he talked to her on the phone at home because his facial expressions showed it. I once tried to rig the answering machine to tape his calls, but it didn't work. I even attempted to follow him but gave up because I felt stupid and knew that if he noticed me, he would think I was crazy. So eventually I rationalized that I didn't have any real evidence and let it go.

Two years went by and even though his pattern didn't change, I knew he was slipping away. I found myself reading my Bible for answers, yet I would lie in bed full of anguish, scared to confront him. But I prayed and held fast that the Lord would work it out.

Finally, I needed to be certain. I went to my cousin and explained to him what had been happening. He seemed to know what to do. First he began following Cole. That's when he got her address and a picture. Then he had a friend who worked for Verizon come to our house and put a recording device in the phone. Two months later he came to me with the evidence. It was then that I took the package, went to my mother's house where I wouldn't be interrupted, and I listened—listened to my husband loving another woman.

COLE

After six months with her, I had to ask myself: What the hell was I doing? I knew that I'd gotten in too deep. When I'd met her I thought she might be fun for a while, like the others had been. Hell, she was single and had her own crib on the other side of town. Just what I needed. I met her driving by on the street. I was walking toward my truck and she was driving past me in her Honda Accord when our eyes met. I mean, I'd caught the eyes of a lot of women on the street but something was different about those eyes.

I motioned for her to pull over and she did, but before I could even turn toward her car, she pulled off again. I figured, what the hell, jumped into my Suburban and began driving down Broad Street. After only a few blocks I saw her making a U-turn in the gas station. I blew my horn and motioned for her to pull over. This time she parked and I knew the shit was on.

When she stepped out of her car in a brown linen suit I was impressed with how tall, slender, and brown she was. Not my usual pick of women, who are light-skinned with long hair and built like shit. No, her hair was natural, full of kinky locs, and she had this look of freedom to her. A little makeup maybe but I really couldn't tell, 'cause I kept looking at her smile. Once we introduced ourselves I could feel my dick start to get hard. Damn, she was fine.

We found a lot to talk about, except for the fact that I was married. I wasn't about to reveal that, not before I at least had a chance to hit that thing. So we rapped for about an hour, more than I usually did with a strange woman, and then she climbed back into her car. As I leaned into the passenger window, she gave me her business card and it was then that I noticed her sliding her sexy foot out of a brown leather mule. Now, I'd always had a foot fetish; shit, I had over one hundred pairs of shoes and probably even more sneaks. But this foot was beautiful and I was anxious to get those toes in my mouth.

I put her card carefully in my pocket, knowing that Sasha was gonna make my August hotter than my July had been.

SASHA

For the first year I didn't even know he was married. A relationship and falling in love were the furthest things from my mind. I'd just gotten out of a relationship three months before I met him, so all I wanted was someone to take the edge off.

My career was moving on fast-forward. I'd just gone from being a secretary, supporting a college dean, to an executive assistant at the high-powered Philadelphia law firm of Mitchell & Ness, whose clients were entertainers and athletes. Suddenly at age thirty-eight I was busier than I'd been as a teen, certainly too busy to realize when Cole wasn't available. Shit, I couldn't help but be attracted to him. He stood six foot four, with a thick 240 pounds spread evenly over him. But more than that, it was the deep black color of his skin that mesmerized me.

Once I found out Cole was married I was simply too caught up to let him go. I'd tried to end it several times, but each time I was pulled back, with him offering me just enough to keep me right there. I often grew tired of living our relationship inside my house and out of state, when he could get away. I wanted us to be normal and he wanted me to be patient. But nothing could take away those lonely Sunday nights when I'd listen to WDAS FM play "Outside Woman," "Saving My Love," "Agony and Ecstasy," "Secret Lover"—*all* the songs that described our relationship.

He kept telling me his wife didn't know anything, didn't even suspect. Having been a wife myself I found that hard to believe, but he insisted. So I figured she was either dumb or didn't care; hell, maybe she had her own thing on the side. Regardless, he was totally unwilling to let me go, yet he was also unwilling to leave his wife, which I'm not even sure I wanted him to do. I didn't want to see him or his family suffer, so instead I endured the suffering.

PAULETTE

It would be easy getting into her house. I'd copied her keys from the extra ring he kept on his key chain.

I took the gun off the seat beside me and carefully placed it in my pocketbook. I looked around before I stepped out of the car and then glanced up to her window to make sure nobody saw me coming. I didn't care that I'd used my own car, nor that I'd parked directly across the street from her house. In the end none of that would matter. The best part was that he had no idea that I knew he was sharing his love with another woman.

As I said a prayer, in an effort to decide if tonight would be my night, the lights went out downstairs, and what appeared to be candlelight began flickering in the bedroom. I hesitated, as the aching in my heart made me want to pound on her door to be let inside. To be let back into the life he'd shut me out of. But no, tonight I would make my move.

I walked past his truck parked in her driveway and onto the porch. Holding the screen door open I slowly inserted the key. I tried the top lock first, but it wasn't locked so I used the doorknob key—it opened. My hands were shaking and I felt sweat beading up between my breasts. I was even more determined. I turned the knob and stepped inside.

I was surprised by the house's simplicity. There were dark-stained hardwood floors that ran throughout the downstairs. The living and dining rooms were covered with Oriental rugs that I'm sure were expensive. I could smell her scent of jasmine and spice and, unexpectedly, I was immediately drawn into Sasha's strange aura, as it had probably drawn in my husband. Yes, I'm sure she had used all of these things to lure my husband away. She was no better than Eve, who had tempted Adam.

The house was quiet except for the television, and then I heard it, the sound of my husband snoring. For fourteen years, I'd listened to that breathing and light choking when he sucked in air too deeply. I started toward the stairs but then changed my mind; first I wanted to see how she lived. See where he was so comfortable over these last five years that he didn't want to be in our home, except to pass through, as if I were the other woman. Why hadn't he ever told me about her, told me he loved someone else, that he wanted a divorce? No, he just silently kept living two lives. I had to stop myself from thinking too much, so I silently prayed.

Her house, though simple, was tastefully furnished. I sat down on a chair in the living room, facing a large-screen television, which I'm sure was his favorite spot, and I guessed that it was probably here that she sat between his legs. But I couldn't get caught up in that, not right now. There were also plants that filled her home, and fresh flowers that stood on a pedestal. And there were pictures of her grandson.

Then I went into the kitchen. This is where she probably pleased him most. My husband loved to eat and I could tell from the smell that she had been baking. There were dishes on the counter, still covered with food: chicken smothered in gravy, rice, salad, and even a fresh-baked apple pie on the counter. I couldn't help but wonder if her food tasted better than mine, so with my fingers I picked a piece of chicken out of the cold gravy and tasted it. Dirty dishes and leftovers, that's how I felt, like a meal he was finished with but couldn't seem to throw away. Well, now he'd have no choice.

I walked back through the dining room, living room and, hesitating at the bottom step, looked up to where all my anguish was coming from. Again, I prayed. As I put my foot on the first step, it squeaked. I held my breath but, realizing it was too late to turn back, I proceeded, one step at a time.

I knew her room was in the front of the house. So once I reached the top step, I held on to the banister to brace myself. There were more family pictures on the wall, and on the table in the hallway there sat a picture of the two of them, laughing and happy. Even though my body cringed, I had to admit they looked in love. But that was my love, my love she'd stolen.

Then I felt it. I felt her sense me, like she knew I'd come. But what she didn't know was what I'd come for. I took the gun from my purse and positioned it firmly in my right hand, removed the safety and placed my finger on the trigger. God will forgive me, I told myself.

Initially I wasn't going to say anything, just do it. But I wanted them to see it happening, and not have a chance to stop me. Approaching the doorway I froze at the sight of the two of them, all cozy and tucked in bed. I wanted to turn away, but no, I was doing the right thing. Hadn't I prayed for this night?

What better way for them to pay? They'd hurt me for so long, and Cole actually thought he was getting away with something. Did he really think I didn't know? For once I would no longer be the good girl. It was my turn to be bad.

COLE

Damn, it felt good to be in bed with her. She had no idea how bad I wished I could just up and leave my family. But no matter how much I thought it through I still came out with the same answer. It was too much work; I had too much to lose. I couldn't walk out on my son, or my wife. Even though our marriage didn't hold any excitement, I still loved Paulette and didn't want to see her hurt. Shit, I even wondered how after all these years she still didn't know. But guess what, I wasn't gonna try to figure it out either. If Paulette could only give me half of what Sasha did, then maybe it would be different at home.

I truly believed Sasha loved me. She knew how to take care of her man. Whatever I needed she'd give to me. Backrubs, baths, dinner on the table when I arrived, TV turned to ESPN, slippers by the door, and sex. Well, I got that any and every way I wanted it. Sometimes it wasn't even the sex, it was just the way she seemed genuinely interested in my life. She believed I could do some of the things I'd lost faith in doing. She was so damn interesting to me; the athletes and celebrities she knew from her job and all that shit she liked: candles, reading, writing, and all that back-to-nature stuff. Sasha wasn't scared of shit. If there was something she wanted to do or try she'd go after it. She had no problem taking risks; hell, I was a risk.

I'd had a lot of women over the years, before and during my marriage, but once me and Sasha hooked up I knew she had me because I hadn't fucked with anybody else. Even though I told her I didn't sleep with my wife, I knew she didn't believe me, but what else could I say? But the sex wasn't the same; lovemaking with Paulette was the same as our marriage—routine. Sasha made me feel like a man. She not only loved me but she loved my body and would examine and make love to every inch of it, even down to my crusty toes. So what was I gonna do—give all this up?

Having Sasha was better than having a wife, 'cause I

knew after being with my wife for fourteen years that wives didn't give that much. They just gave enough to stay married. That's why I also knew that as much as she wanted me here, if I were to come, to move in, she would change. She'd get comfortable and feel like she didn't have to treat me special anymore. As long as the relationship stayed like this, I could be with her forever and then maybe one day, when my son graduated high school, I could make a move. And she knew; she knew I wasn't leaving and didn't often ask except those times when she wanted me so bad she couldn't take it anymore. I knew I was selfish but the way things were is what worked for me.

Sasha did deserve more—deserved a man who could be there with her in the morning and be able to count on him coming home every night, someone she could feel like number one with. But what she didn't know is that she was number one with me. I couldn't let her go; I couldn't let her give anybody else what she'd given me. So lying here tonight, after having been drenched in her love, I was in my comfort zone. The way she lay tucked underneath me like a finished puzzle made me know that she felt the same way.

SASHA

I knew she'd come. No matter how much he denied she had knowledge of us, I knew eventually she would let us know she was no real fool. So here we were, the three of us. Even with the gun in her hand we just stared at each other, knowing it had come to this. I could see through the dimness of the evening light that Paulette was sadly beautiful.

Who would she shoot, Cole or me? Who would she

hold to blame, Cole, because he was her husband, the one who'd stood before God and made the commitment? Or me, because she thought I was some whore breaking up their marriage? I still couldn't move. I called Cole's name, watched his body slowly turn, saw his face look at her, look at me, and before I could answer the question in his eyes . . .

COLE

I know Sasha thought I was sleeping, but her squirming had already woke me, so when she called my name I didn't answer right away. Then I felt Sasha nudge me and I heard my name being called again but this time it was my wife's voice. I turned over to make sure I was hearing right, and there she stood. What the fuck was my wife doing in Sasha's bedroom doorway?

As my eyes adjusted to the darkness, I could see that not only was my wife there, but she was holding my fucking 9-millimeter in her hand. I looked from Sasha to Paulette to ask what the fuck was going on, but before I could say anything, before I could even explain, as if there would be an explanation why I was in another woman's bed, the gun went off.

PAULETTE

Sasha and I never took our eyes off each other while she called his name, and when he didn't respond, I called him. He moved, he turned, looked at me, looked at her, and, before he could ask any questions, I pulled the trigger.

1

CRIME SCENE

Before Cole could get out of bed he had to slap me to stop my screaming. Paulette had shot herself at close range through the head. He grabbed my face tightly, pushed the phone into my hand, and shouted for me to call 911. I dialed the number while Cole fell to the floor cradling Paulette's body as if he could push the pieces of her back together.

The police dispatcher tried to keep me rational by asking numerous questions.

Tears filled my eyes as I tried to explain.

"What's your name, ma'am?"

"Sasha Borianni."

"Where do you live?" she asked.

I gave her my address.

"Ms. Borianni, is the person still breathing?"

"I don't know," I answered, even though my instincts told me Paulette was dead.

"How long ago did it happen?"

I noticed my watch on the nightstand and fastened it to my wrist.

"Damn it, it just happened!" I yelled, tears choking my throat.

"Is the scene safe?" she asked in a very monotone voice.

"Yeah." I could feel myself fading away.

"Who shot her?" she asked.

"She did it," I whispered.

"I don't understand? Is the gun still there?" She hesitated, waiting for my reply. "Ma'am, do you know the victim?"

Did I? I silently wondered.

Frustrated with her questions, I cried, "Could you just please hurry up and send some help?"

I hung up the phone, realizing that I had to phone Amir, Cole's brother. Cole had always told me to call Amir if I ever needed to get in touch with Cole in case of an emergency. I'm sure neither of us would've imagined me calling his brother under these circumstances. While I explained the story of Paulette's suicide, Amir remained quiet and only asked where his brother was.

Within minutes I heard sirens rushing toward my home and saw flashing red lights reflecting off my windows. Then, the doorbell rang. Realizing I was naked, I pulled on Cole's tee shirt, which was lying on the floor. I ran downstairs to the front door where two policemen identified themselves and asked what had happened. I could see an ambulance and paramedics running up the driveway and police cars coming from both ends of my one-way street.

"Who's here with you?" The white officer asked while peering at my half-naked body.

"Me and Cole," I answered, as if he knew us.

"Is it safe to come in the house?"

I nodded my head yes and pointed upstairs. "He's with her. He's holding her."

At this point his Hispanic partner spoke into his radio, giving various code names and numbers, but it was clear he was contacting the Homicide Division.

The white officer asked, while opening his notebook, "What's your full name, ma'am?"

"Sasha Borianni."

"And the man's name?"

"Cole Allen."

"His wife?"

"Paulette Allen."

Unsure of the circumstances, the cop had me follow him up the steps to my bedroom. Holding the cordless phone, I stood in the hallway while two officers and the paramedics trailed us. The cops cautiously entered my bedroom, being careful not to disturb anything. One cop slowly moved toward Cole and eased Paulette from his arms while the other officer bent down to check the pulse in Paulette's neck and wrist. The look they gave each other confirmed that she was dead. The paramedics began hopelessly trying to resuscitate Paulette, I guess because it was their job to at least try. But their efforts were wasted and within minutes they pronounced her dead. Cole just sat on the floor staring right through all that was happening.

Before I could go to Cole, a man and woman came through the doorway. He introduced himself as Detective

Rankins from the Homicide Division and his partner as
Detective Stiles. I could tell by the way she looked me
over that Detective Stiles detested me. I looked at her
hand and noticed that she was married and I knew why.
As Rankins looked me up and down in my state of half-
nakedness, he asked me if I'd like to put some clothes on,
which seemed to piss Stiles off. Unable to speak, I nodded
my head yes. I pulled my sweatpants from the floor where
Cole had just hours ago stripped them from me. Stiles
motioned for me to follow her into the bathroom as she
eerily watched me get dressed.

Before I could finish dressing, someone yelled from my
bedroom.

"Yo, Stiles, we need some help in here!"

I ran behind Stiles to my room where Cole, still naked,
was bending over his wife's body, which the coroner was
inspecting like a dead animal. I noticed they'd covered
their shoes with plastic booties and inserted Paulette's
hands into brown paper bags. I also noticed they'd placed
the gun into a plastic bag. Cole was splattered with blood
from his thighs to his waist. Two officers were practically
dragging him out of the room and down the hallway. I
began to get angry, "Can he at least get some clothes on?"
I asked.

"Sure, ma'am," Rankins said.

"Well, they're on the chair in my room!"

Another officer passed me the clothes as he led Cole
downstairs, followed by Rankins and Stiles.

Once they had Cole downstairs, sitting in what was his
favorite chair, I went to him but he turned away from me.
Rankins told me it was best if I stayed in the other room.
I could tell they were trying to keep us apart, but I

couldn't figure out why. I assumed they thought we had a different story to tell, but it didn't matter because Cole wasn't talking. I stood watching Cole from the kitchen doorway, a broken man. His entire body was limp and he wasn't even able to hold his head up. Never having seen him cry, I watched tears stream from his eyes, as over and over he repeated, "Allah, what have I done?"

The next official people to come through the door were from the crime lab. Detective Rankins went back upstairs and gave orders that it was okay to enter the "crime scene." A chill shot through my body like somebody had pumped crushed ice through my veins, and I began to shake. I could hear the officers talking about "sifting through evidence" and "collecting fibers" and everything began to get clear.

There were so many policemen and detectives in the house that I felt as if I'd stepped into a movie. They had filled my home and quickly cordoned off my bedroom with yellow tape that read "crime scene" in black letters. I could hear the cops outside talking to the ones in the house on walkie-talkies, trying to secure the scene. Everyone knew their role, as one officer took pictures and another spoke into a tape recorder, giving details of what was now officially the crime scene.

I wasn't sure why—maybe it was because I needed something to focus on—but I became obsessed with checking my watch. It was 11:00 P.M. It couldn't have been more than an hour since I'd first called 911. I watched and listened as they brought down bags of evidence and took them outside to the black-and-white crime scene vehicle. Paulette's body remained in the house, and I overheard one of the policemen say, "She'll be the last to go because the coroner hasn't finished yet."

But still I wanted to be strong, hold on to some dignity with all these strangers in my house. It was then that Stiles spoke up and announced that we'd have to go downtown to give a statement.

Rankins and Stiles then began hustling Cole and me along to separate cars, taking us to Police Headquarters, at 8th and Race Streets, usually referred to by Philadelphians as the Roundhouse because of its shape. When they escorted us outside I noticed that the television news vans had showed up. The police were able to hold them back because they'd marked my house off with barricades. I also noticed that Amir was waiting outside. The police hadn't allowed him to enter the house. I told Rankins who he was and he sent an officer to tell Amir to meet us at the Roundhouse.

My life had now become a spectacle for all. I had nothing to shield my face from the onlookers so I just kept my head down. In doing so, I noticed that someone had trampled my recently sprouted flower bed of pansies and tulips lining the driveway.

Arriving at the Roundhouse, we found Cole's mother and attorney waiting. Cole's mother charged toward me, filled with rage, as if I were the one who'd pulled the trigger. Before she could reach me, Amir grabbed her arm and led her away. But I still heard her hateful words, "Bitch, look what you've done. You've killed my son's wife!"

I felt Rankins's eyes on me, and without looking at his face, I could tell he pitied me. Maybe he thought I'd killed Paulette to get Cole. But no, he'd been nice to me and seemed to believe everything I'd told him. It was

Stiles and the other cops who had snooped around through things that had nothing to do with what had happened. They had poked into what I thought was a relationship but would now be known as nothing more than a sordid affair.

My strength was waning because I knew that what Cole's mother had said was true. My selfishness and greedy need to love Paulette's husband had surely pushed her over the edge and caused her death. If only I'd alerted Cole when I'd first heard the noise, maybe Paulette would still be alive. I needed to call somebody, I couldn't do this alone. I asked to phone my attorney—not that I had one, but I knew Mitchell, the entertainment lawyer I worked for, would come to the station. At this request Stiles, in her bitchiest voice, asked. "Now why would you wanna do that? You guilty of something?" I knew it was better to keep my mouth shut because she had me at her mercy, but Rankins spoke up. "Leave her alone, Stiles."

It took Mitchell an hour to get there and fortunately they gave us some time alone. He'd met Cole on numerous occasions but had no idea that he was a married man. After telling him what had happened, I asked him to call the three people who were closest to me: my son Owen in California, my daddy, and my best friend, Arshell, who lived in Maryland.

Then the questioning began. "Now, Ms. Borianni, can you please tell me again the chain of events?" Rankins asked.

All of a sudden things had taken on new names. I hesitated at first, thinking of my rights, but realizing I hadn't shot anyone, I told him how Paulette had appeared in my bedroom doorway.

"What time did you first hear the noise?" asked Rankins.

"Why didn't you wake Mr. Allen? How long have you two been having an affair?" chimed in Stiles before I could answer the first question.

Rankins continued, "What time did it happen? What were you doing at the time?"

All of a sudden Rankins didn't seem to be so nice anymore.

"Did she see you having sex?" Stiles kept digging. "C'mon, Ms. Borianni, I'm sure you realized that it would be much easier for you and Mr. Allen to be together with his wife out the way."

Then it was Rankins's turn. "You really want me to believe that you didn't want Ms. Allen out of the way?"

My emotions were boiling over. I stuttered in answering their questions because they were coming too fast. I screamed. "She committed suicide. Can't you fuckin' tell?!"

Then Mitchell spoke up. "Excuse me, detectives, but if you're not charging my client with anything then I ask that she be free to go."

I thought maybe this was just a movie I was caught in.

After six hours of their grueling questions and checks into my background, I was finally free to go. As much as I wanted to keep my head up, my eyes were burning from crying, along with the sun beating down on me as we walked to Mitchell's car.

Arriving back at my house, there were still a few police cars and reporters lurking about. I could see my neighbors standing on their front lawns talking with one another and I was sure the cops had questioned them, since many of them had met Cole and seen him come and go over the last five years. The people of Chestnut Hill certainly weren't used to the publicity they were being exposed to. I had tainted my neighborhood's cobblestone streets and quaint shops with blood.

Inside the house, Daddy sat on the couch fidgeting with the TV remote control, unable to even find the power button. I'd never seen him like that. He didn't say much, just motioned for me to sit next to him. Mitchell explained in detail what had occurred and I watched as creases formed across Daddy's forehead.

"What do we need to do, Mitchell?" Daddy asked.

"Just hold tight. I have a friend who can probably handle this."

"What's there to handle? She killed herself, right?" he asked, glancing at me for reassurance. Mitchell didn't wait for me to respond.

"Yes, but they'll want to investigate some more to make sure there was no foul play, and I just want to make sure Sasha's rights are protected."

Through the screen door I noticed a cab pulling up carrying Owen, who'd obviously taken the red eye flight from Los Angeles. He ignored reporters, nosy neighbors, and police. I stepped into the doorway to meet him and Owen immediately took me into his young arms.

"Mom, what happened?" He'd known about Cole for the last few years and had been on me to leave him alone. He'd insisted that I deserved more, but now I reasoned in my head that I was probably getting what I deserved.

"Owen, I'm sorry. It wasn't my fault," I cried.

My mind was drained and my body beaten. We sat in the kitchen—me, Mitchell, and Owen—nobody knowing the right words to say.

Mitchell went through the story again, but I could tell Owen wanted to hear from me. But every time I tried to talk, tried to make it right, make some sense out of the nightmare I was living, tears choked the words out of me. So I gave up. Mitchell made a few phone calls and then announced he was leaving. I walked him to the door, apologizing and thanking him at the same time. Outside I noticed that everyone had gone and the streets where children usually played were empty.

The house grew quiet, with my father lying on the couch while Owen stood scraping away our leftovers and washing the dishes. Finally I found the courage to ask Owen to go upstairs with me. I had to see.

From the end of the hallway I could see the chalk outline of where Paulette's body had been. Then there was the blood; it had touched everything. It wasn't just on my hardwood floors, but had splattered on my soft yellow walls and bedding. There was debris scattered around the room from the police investigation—multiple pairs of rubber gloves the police had used in examining her and paper and plastic wrappers from the different instruments.

"Why didn't the police clean up?" I asked Owen. He didn't bother to answer, just stepped into the bedroom and looked around, with me following close behind.

"Mom, I'll clean it up," he said.

I couldn't move. I leaned against the wall and stared at the shape of her, wondering about the type of person she'd been. Cole and I rarely discussed her. Then it hit me—Cole's son had also lost his mother. What had I done? Maybe I had killed her. At that moment I wanted her to return to my doorway so I could apologize for loving her husband.

I hadn't noticed that Owen had left the room until I saw him return with a mop, sponges, and a bucket filled with hot water and Lysol. He kept insisting that I go downstairs so he could clean up. I ignored him and reached into the bucket, squeezed out the mop and began mopping up her blood, while Owen took a sponge and started cleaning the blood speckles off the walls. As I put the mop back into the bucket, I watched the water turn pink and I began to cry, just a few tears at first and then racking sobs. I was so distraught Owen had to grab me because my legs were buckling. It felt like my bones were detaching from each other. My knees hit the floor and I fell, fell down into her blood that was now mixed with water and tears. Through my blurred eyes I could see that not only was her blood on the floor, but brown pieces of what had probably been Paulette were also there.

"No, no!" I screamed. "This can't be happening! Why couldn't she have killed me? I was the one who deserved to die. Cole, I'm so sorry."

I was so hysterical that Owen yelled for his grandfather. The two of them picked me up and laid me in bed, which only made it worse because I could smell Cole and the scent of our sex from just hours before.

Owen begged, "Mom, please don't do this to yourself."

"Sasha, Sasha!" My father screamed, trying to get through to me.

Then I heard Arshell calling my name. I heard her running up the stairs, then she ran into the room, moving Owen and Daddy out of the way to reach me. Arshell ordered Owen to get a glass of water, pulled a container of pills from her purse, told me to open my mouth, and inserted two Xanax. "I can't lie here. Please, Arshell, I can still smell them. She's still here."

"Nobody's here, Sasha, but your family."

"Arshell, it's all my fault," I kept repeating, as she held me and rocked me until I finally fell into a fitful sleep.

The next morning I woke up horrified that I'd fallen asleep in my room. At first I wasn't even sure what day it was, but looking at my watch I saw it was ten in the morning. Lying beside me was Owen. Even in sleep I could see that my son felt powerless over the life his mother had chosen to live.

I climbed out of bed and saw that the blood had been cleaned up, but I could still smell it. Paulette's suicide smelled like raw chicken gone bad. I went to the bathroom where I coughed and gagged, trying to throw up, but nothing came out. I sat on the side of the tub and turned on the water, but I didn't have the strength to take a shower. I yearned for Cole at that very moment. I needed him to make me understand what had happened over the last two days. Knowing he was farther out of my grasp then he'd ever been, I instead pulled on my bathrobe, a present from Cole, and went downstairs to the comforting sound of Arshell's voice. She was hanging up the phone as I entered the kitchen.

"Listen, Mitchell called. He's getting you a criminal attorney."

"What do I need a lawyer for? I didn't do anything."

"Look, Sasha, this is what you have to understand. The cops know it was a suicide, but they could easily switch this shit up and blame it on you and Cole."

Arshell turned away from me but I noticed from the movement of her shoulders that she was crying. I went to her, wrapping my arms around her waist. There we stood, the both of us, weeping over the affair that had ended Paulette's life.

"And Sasha, there's more."

"What is it?" I asked, not even sure I wanted to know.

"You can't talk to Cole," she said, almost in a whisper.

"What? What do you mean?" I dropped my arms from around her and she turned to face me.

"You are not to see him. You are not to talk to him until this shit is over, so don't try any dumb shit. You hear me?"

I finally understood. Not only had Paulette taken her own life, but she'd taken mine too.

2

ROOTS

June 1998

As the days passed and everyone returned to their lives, Arshell to Maryland and Owen to California, my life strayed further and further from normal. It seemed everywhere I went in Philly people stared at me. Like they knew I was a dirty whore who'd slept with a married man whose wife had killed herself. The local news kept the scandal and relationship alive long after it stopped breathing. I'd even received threatening phone calls from supposed "church sisters" of Paulette's.

Too many nights I cried on the phone to Arshell about my horrible existence. She was in constant contact with me, telling me things to keep me strong that she probably didn't even believe. About how it wasn't my fault and how Paulette had to be twisted to take her own life over a man.

Arshell was practically insisting that I come down and stay with her and her family in Maryland, and on more than one occasion she suggested I relocate and start over elsewhere. But that was typical Arshell, always trying to find a way to make things better when a situation looks bad.

I tried to stay away from everyone I knew and only answered those calls that were really important. I certainly wasn't taking any calls from reporters. Even my extended family and limited friends who phoned couldn't get through to me. I mean, why were they calling anyway? Just to be nosy, to come over to see the spot in the room where Paulette had blown out her brains.

So when I shopped for groceries I did it outside the neighborhood, my hairdresser was kind enough to book my appointments on off hours, and when I did see folks I knew I nodded in greeting and kept going, avoiding all conversation. I'm sure any information they needed the media would have been happy to provide. Hell, they'd interviewed people going back to my playground days. Was I lonely? Yes. So my time was spent either in the house or I'd work in my yard with my back to my neighbors.

Most every morning, though, I was awakened by images of Paulette laughing at me. I'd taken to sleeping on the futon on my sun porch where Cole and I had spent many summer evenings because I couldn't bring myself to return to my bedroom. On these nights I would sit up reading the diary my long-deceased mother had written while she was pregnant with me. Most of it was abstract sentences, but she had definitely been happy to be pregnant. She hadn't known whether I'd be a boy or girl, but she'd intended on loving me and teaching me strong values. Daddy didn't like to talk about my mother much but reminded me that she died giving birth to me. I think this made me feel more guilty than anything else.

Judging by my current circumstances, I guessed I needed the love and life lessons in my mother's diary. Not that Daddy hadn't tried, but he was certainly lacking in emotional availability. However, there were things that Daddy had given to me. Even though it was just the two of us, Daddy made me feel like we were a complete family. Daddy said there had been a lot of naysayers when Mommy died who said he couldn't take care of a baby or raise a little girl by himself, but he was determined to prove them wrong.

Mealtime was important to Daddy, as it was usually then when he would talk about my mother. He would tell me how patient she'd always been with him, yet when she wanted her way she would make her demands, leaving him no recourse but to say yes.

Even then Daddy still missed her cooking, so he began to teach me at age ten how to fry chicken and make potato salad, two staples he said a Black woman must always know how to cook. When his memories of my mother would overwhelm him, he'd just say, "Well, Sasha, it's just me and you now."

I always felt like Daddy's little princess and I knew he gave me extra love because I was all he had. I was the only woman he could trust, he said. Daddy, as he insisted I always refer to him, made it known that when I became a woman I was never to call another man by that name, that he was the only man worthy of that title.

Daddy was employed as a limousine driver and I spent a lot of time riding quietly in the front seat while he drove people with money around to places we never entered. He was always explaining the importance of money and the things it could buy. At Christmas he gave me boxes of clothes and toys that I hadn't even asked for. On Valentine's Day there were hearts filled with chocolate and always a jewelry trinket. His gifts weren't expensive, but he needed a way to show his love.

His grandmother had been a full-blooded Italian. He held little resemblance to her but made sure I knew my heritage. Daddy didn't know a lot about Italy but he knew a helluva lot about the Mafia, even if most of it was from television. He owned the entire *Godfather* series and any other movie that carried a mob storyline. I grew up between North Philly and West Philly where there weren't a lot of Italians but there was a lot of Black culture.

But there was another side of him. Daddy enjoyed gambling. He wasn't obsessed but he loved a good card game and was always comparing life and its events to a deck of cards. Most especially, he often repeated, "Sasha, don't ever let anybody see your full hand."

He constantly told me as I grew up that I had to be tough, to be strong, that I couldn't be soft like most women. When I complained about not having a mother, he would reply, "You can't miss what you never had." But I did, even though I pretended it didn't bother me—especially when I'd see other little girls dressed up with their mothers fussing over them. I had no idea what it felt like to call somebody Mommy, and would often practice those words in the mirror, like if I said them hard enough and long enough my mother might appear. No matter how long I practiced, she never came.

When Daddy did go out, I'd spend that time with my mother's sister, who was good to me but couldn't be good herself. I hated my Aunt Lou for continually allowing herself to be abused by Ernest, her no-good funky-smelling boyfriend. When I would spend the night, I'd listen to her cries as she was beaten and then forced to have sex. I couldn't understand why one moment she'd be screaming at him to stop hitting her and then the next she'd be moaning in pleasure. As always, the following morning she'd school me on how men had problems and needed to be understood. All I understood at the time was that sex was used to somehow make pain disappear, I supposed just the same way a kiss made a child's bruises feel better. Maybe it was the same with adults?

According to Daddy, Sasha meant "protector of men," and he constantly reminded me that I had to protect him. It was my job to protect Daddy from his women getting too close. He never let another woman live with us—they barely spent the night and I certainly kept them out of our kitchen.

Daddy thought that I needed to know how to be a good woman to a man and how not to let one take advantage of me. "They gotta pay the cost to be the boss," he'd say, when I'd talk to him about boys. He insisted that a man should always have something to offer me because what they wanted in return was too precious to give away.

I realized early on that sex was a priority for men. And that women *and* money were what satisfied Daddy. He would bring women home often after I'd gone to bed, and sex seemed to always make those women happy. I wanted that happiness, too. I would sometimes peek downstairs and catch him having sex. I couldn't believe that a woman could make my Daddy look weak. They did things to him that, at the time, I thought were disgusting. But afterward, he'd return to the same strong man I always thought he was. Like he had no idea that he'd just been in another place. I envied those women who could control a man with sex and vowed that one day I would possess that same control.

3

ROOKIE

August 1998

It had been almost four months since the tragedy and there was the lingering possibility of a civil trial. Paulette's family was suing me and Cole in civil court. The charge was "intentional infliction of emotional distress—wrongful death." There were several meetings with my criminal attorney, Joel Senquinni, who needed to know all the details of my relationship with Cole. There was also the issue of custody. Paulette's mother was fighting with Cole for his son. And from what I heard, Cole Jr. wanted to be with his grandmother.

I hadn't returned to work, so the only activity I had was my volunteer work at the Morris Arboretum where, thankfully, no one bothered me. So I'd go there and cry among the living plants and flowers, sometimes wishing I could bury myself in the dirt among them.

Mitchell, to finally lure me out of my shame and back to work, decided to present me with what he called "the opportunity of a lifetime." It seemed one of Mitchell's clients, a twenty-three-year-old NBA All-Star named Phoenix Carter, who played center for Chicago, was in need of a personal assistant. I vaguely knew Phoenix through a few phone conversations while waiting for Mitchell to pick up the line, but for the most part I'd kept my distance from all the celebrity clients.

I didn't want to get too excited, but it did sound interesting. So I did a little research to see exactly who this Phoenix Carter was. It didn't take much. After a little surfing for articles on the Internet and a few episodes on ESPN, I could see he was an arrogant thug who was followed around by at least ten of his friends, his eyes hidden under a baseball cap. His voice was barely audible when speaking to the media; I assumed he was trying to be cool, as was the way of this new breed of athletes who didn't marry white girls and didn't take well to the rules of the NBA.

Phoenix had been in a few minor scuffs with the law but nothing major. The interesting thing was that he was twenty years old when he'd graduated high school, which made it look like he'd either been held back just long enough to win the school championship or maybe the kid had been a slow starter. The more I thought about it, the more it seemed like a bigger job than I might want to take on. I was in no way eager to raise another child.

But I had to admit that regardless of Phoenix Carter's rough edges he was probably as handsome as they came at such a young age. As I watched him make cameos in the music videos I rented, I could see why any young woman would be after him.

Mitchell informed me that Phoenix would be phoning him later in the week so we could set up a meeting to discuss the details. He wanted to get everything settled before the season opened in November. From the sound of things, it looked like I didn't have a choice because Mitchell and Phoenix had already decided my new career for me.

It was a Thursday morning when Phoenix phoned and I made reservations at The Striped Bass for the three of us. Driving in the ninety-two-degree Philly humidity, I cursed myself for not getting the air conditioner in my car repaired. But my mechanic now knew too many details of my life. I was anxious enough at the thought of meeting Phoenix Carter; now I'd be all sweaty and wrinkled when I arrived. I'd gone shopping to be prepared and wore a salmon-colored linen skirt suit from Toby Lerner's and a pair of strappy cream-colored Enzo sandals. My hair was pulled on top of my head with just a few locs draping my face. My intentions weren't to flirt with the young man, but he was still a man and I had to look good. I'd learned long ago that regardless of the feminist movement and women wanting to be equal to men, we still used our sex appeal when necessary to secure an opportunity.

Stepping into the air-conditioned vestibule, I took a few minutes to gather myself. I decided to leave my sunglasses on until I sat down. As I approached the table, they both stood up and I couldn't help but notice the way Phoenix looked me over.

"Hello, Sasha. You look great. Very well rested,"

Mitchell said, as he pulled my chair out and seated me across from Phoenix but close enough to where he had a full view of me. "Please have a seat."

He looked at Phoenix, whose eyes were locked on me.

"Sasha Borianni, Phoenix Carter."

"It's my pleasure, Mr. Carter."

He nodded his head up and down, reached across the table, and shook my hand. I removed my glasses to get a better look at him.

This Phoenix Carter was a showstopper in person, practically captivating. Maybe he wasn't as thugged-out as I thought, but I couldn't tell because there were so many other things to take in about this young phenom.

"Yeah, Mitchell was right. You do look good. So, what's up?"

Before I could answer, the waitress came over to take my drink order but her eyes stayed on Phoenix.

His appearance didn't go unnoticed by the restaurant's occupants either. How could it? He seemed to fill up the restaurant with his presence. The manager of the restaurant asked to take a picture with him and there were a few autograph seekers, mostly grown-ass businessmen claiming to want his autograph for their children. Yes, young Phoenix Carter possessed a certain charisma that impressed me.

Surprisingly, I found myself getting aroused to the point where I could feel my panties begin to get wet. I wasn't sure if it had been that long since I'd taken the time to look at a man, or if it was Phoenix himself who had me turned on. I mean, here he was, a muscular six-foot-nine-inches tall and about 280 pounds; he definitely had the center of my attention. Phoenix looked very comfortable in his Timberland boots, Guess? denim shorts that hung low enough to reveal the waistband of his Polo underwear, a wife-beater, and a shiny bald head to top it off.

But I mostly couldn't help looking at his glittering jewelry. Everything was encased in platinum. His necklace was filled with diamonds—ice, as they called it— from which hung a diamond cross. Then there was a large diamond ring, diamond hoop earrings, and what had to be a custom-made platinum and diamond Rolex watch. He was a walking millionaire, surely the closest I'd ever been to one.

"So, what do you think you can do for me?"

"I'm hoping you'll tell me what you need. I believe that's why we're here," I answered, then glanced down at my menu.

Mitchell took over. "Exactly. Now what Phoenix is looking for is for you to basically handle his business affairs, public image, and schedule his off-court appearances."

"Yeah, my shit is outta order," he said as I pretended not to notice him rocking back in his chair and grabbing hold of his dick.

"Well, I'm sure we can fix that. Why don't I tell you my background and we'll see if I'm what you're looking for."

After sipping my lemon water I began my spiel, but he stopped me halfway through.

"Hold up. You can stop all that. Sounds like you got the skills, so when you wanna start?"

We both looked at Mitchell, who then began to rattle off the details. He shocked the hell out of me by offering me $75K with the option to negotiate a new salary after the first year. I'd continue to get health and 401K benefits from Mitchell & Ness until we were able to establish Phoenix's business entity. This was almost too much for me at one time. Hell, in addition to having a sexy new boss, I was getting a $20K raise.

With the business side done, Mitchell suggested we talk about our personal lives since we'd be working so close. Phoenix was engaged and had two children. He was originally from Sarasota, Florida, but had made his home in Chicago, where he'd been playing since he'd left high school two years ago. He kept houses in Chicago and Florida but also had a brownstone in Brooklyn for when he just wanted to chill. I could only guess what that meant. Surprisingly, he wasn't the product of a broken home; he had two younger brothers and had been raised by both his parents: His mother was a nurse and his father owned a construction company.

I talked about myself and shared with him that I'd grown up with my dad, my mom having died in child-birth. I told him about my son, Owen, who was twenty-one and lived in L.A. with his wife and new baby. I saw a look of surprise cross his face.

"I know I'm not supposed to ask a woman this shit, but how old are you?"

"It doesn't bother me. I'm thirty-eight," I answered, proud that I still looked good at my age despite the drama I'd been through.

"Damn. What you do to look like that?" he asked, his eyes slowly taking in every inch of me before continuing. "Somebody must be taking real good care of you."

I paused before answering, thinking that my body hadn't seen any action since Cole. But there was more than one way to reply to his question, so I said, "Well, I guess I eat pretty healthy and when I feel like it I walk about three miles a day."

He complimented me on my locs and told me they were the best he'd seen. I had to fight the urge to compliment his sculpted arms and long thick fingers. Then Phoenix did what people usually didn't do—he questioned my last name, Borianni. It never seemed to stand out since all Blacks had white folks' last names.

I told him what little I knew about my Italian background, but pointed out that my knack for cooking Italian cuisine proved my heritage. I was startled when Mitchell attested to my skill in the kitchen. I was so lost in Phoenix I forgot he was there. Cooking pasta sauce from scratch came to me as easy as frying chicken, and I definitely made the best lasagna. Even with this, I never boasted about my Italian heritage. What was the point? I was a Black woman. So with that, Phoenix made me promise that one day I'd fix him an authentic Italian dish.

With Mitchell's coaxing I briefly told Phoenix about the tragedy that had occurred in my life. I told him I'd be keeping a low profile during the civil trial so it shouldn't affect our working relationship. His only question was "Are you still seeing that nigga?" For the first time, I was glad when I honestly answered "No."

But I missed Cole and hadn't spoken to him since Paulette's suicide, which increased the pain and guilt I already felt. Even sitting there being turned on by Phoenix Carter, a young stallion in his own right, my mind never lingered far from Cole. The thought of seeing him again or hearing his voice was probably what kept me going. I knew that no matter what happened, one day he'd reach out to me. If he didn't, then maybe he really hadn't loved me after all.

Phoenix was eager to get started and offered me a $10K signing bonus, an American Express card, and access to a bank account with enough money to cover what would soon be enormous startup costs. He immediately pushed me to purchase whatever I needed to get his business organized and running smoothly. I was overwhelmed that a person could move this fast and offer so much money, but I wasn't about to turn it down.

So I accepted. Suddenly I was the personal assistant to an NBA athlete. Hell, the brother was only twenty-three, so how much trouble could he be? I had a son almost that age.

I had to make a few calls—Arshell, Owen, and Daddy—to share the news. They were thrilled for me, but a bit concerned about how many game tickets they could get. When Arshell said, "Sasha, listen to me," I knew she was about to mother me. Arshell knew my history with men and lay down the law. "You cannot fuck anyone in or around the NBA. I don't care how hot and wet you get, even if it's running down your legs, take a towel and wipe it up. Just don't make that mistake." I promised I wouldn't and assured her I just wanted to make some money. After my past history, the last thing I wanted was a man. More important, I was eager to move past the memories of Paulette and Cole. What Arshell didn't know, and what I didn't tell her, was that I was curious about what it'd be like to get with Phoenix.

On my first business trip for Phoenix, I traveled to New York to meet his fiancée, Crystal. Before leaving, Mitchell warned me not to become friends with her or any of the other NBA wives. Crystal was young, nineteen, with two little boys, ages two and six months. She was a gorgeous young girl, petite with brown skin and long wavy hair. She had hopes of going to college after the kids started school. Crystal and Phoenix appeared to have a solid relationship, and had been together since high school, so I didn't understand why he hadn't married her yet. She wasted no time telling me that she was quite aware of the many women that floated in and out of Phoenix's life. I wasn't sure if she was telling me this for my benefit or for hers. She did, though, reassure me that at no time would she ask me to divulge anything that I'd seen or heard Phoenix do. For that I was glad.

Two weeks later I was ordering equipment to begin setting up a workspace in my home and in Phoenix's house in Chicago. I had no idea what I was supposed to do as his personal assistant, so I just played it like a secretary and followed his lead. He kept telling people. "Talk to her, she's my assistant," and soon people began asking me if they could schedule interviews and if Phoenix would consider endorsing their products or events. It seemed the more celebrity Phoenix gained, the less money he spent—and that's what Phoenix liked. He was also teaching me to reap the benefits of his celebrity.

Phoenix's goal was to make money outside of basketball by learning the world of finance. As he so simply put it, he wanted to learn about anything that had to do with his money. To jump-start his business, Phoenix also wanted me to be aggressive and go after deals that interested him. He didn't just want his own sneaker or a Sprite commercial. He wanted big deals from Microsoft to Mercedes with a few investments thrown in for good measure.

It was clear that my days of sitting in an office answering phones were over.

Mitchell set up Phoenix's corporation, Carter Enterprises, and based it in Chicago. Initially I was the lone employee. But over the next few months my life turned into a circus. It seemed my cell phone and laptop were connected to me at the hip. Since Phoenix didn't have an agent, Mitchell reviewed all his contracts. Now he wanted me to be the first point of contact for anyone trying to get to him. I decided that the best way to let people know I worked for Phoenix Carter was to be seen. And Mitchell began to tell people that if they wanted any piece of Phoenix, they had to talk to me.

I was at Phoenix's side during all of his entertainment appearances—MTV and BET interviews, record-label events, and music videos where rappers wanted his cameo appearance. Soon my name quickly became attached to Phoenix Carter. I was enjoying it all, meeting celebrities that I'd only seen on television, never letting on that I was impressed by anyone.

I was truly in the fast lane. Phoenix promised me, though, that once the season started, things would slow down. But for now, he had to have his last bit of fun. At my suggestion, his entourage eventually whittled down to include his bodyguard, three friends, and, of course, me wedged somewhere in between. And there were women, Black, white, Hispanic, young, old, and they were *everywhere*. Sometimes Phoenix would be with more than one woman a night. I didn't know where he got the stamina. But it wasn't my job to question his endurance—I noticed the goings-on and kept my mouth shut.

The first time Phoenix offered me a perk, we were

shopping in Beverly Hills after a two-day commercial shoot for Nike. I'd planned on visiting my son and his family, but they'd gone to Mexico on vacation. Phoenix and I had spent most of the time between a luxury trailer and a tattoo studio where the commercial was being shot. On this particular afternoon we'd gone shopping on Rodeo Drive. It was ridiculous, the ease with which he spent money on himself and others.

"Is this how you always shop? Just in and out buying what you want while someone else carries the bags?" I asked, noticing that he carried nothing but a platinum card, which he rarely used because he had an account in almost every store.

"Why shouldn't I? It ain't like I don't have the money."

"I guess."

"Check this out, Sasha. If you had my money, you'd do the same thing. What else is there to do with it? Hell, I can't invest all of it. I gotta have some fun. You should try having fun sometimes."

I was offended. "What makes you think I don't?"

He stopped outside the door of Barney's, put his hands on my shoulders and leaned into me.

"You think I can't tell your mind is still on that shit that happened back in Philly? I may be young but I ain't stupid. Plus, if you were having fun out here in L.A. you wouldn't be spending so much time with me."

I was speechless. He let go of my shoulders and stepped around me to take a photo with two young kids. Was it that obvious that I still thought about Cole and suffered behind Paulette's death? Had I allowed myself to become absorbed in someone else's life to hide from my own?

I lagged behind as we entered Barney's but noticed him sizing me up as he started looking at women's clothes.

"C'mon, Sasha. Time for you to do some shopping."

I protested at first, but he insisted, so I let him purchase a Gucci briefcase and a pair of Manolo Blahnik shoes for me. It was impossible to deny him.

Later that evening, after checking in with Daddy, I phoned Arshell.

"Hey, woman of the world. What's happening? Where are you?"

"Beverly Hills with Phoenix."

"What's wrong? You don't sound good."

"Arshell, do I not have a life? Do I seem that miserable to you?"

"What are you talking about? You're fine. You have a great job, you're making fantastic money. What else would a girl want?"

"A life like yours would be nice. You know, a husband and kids."

"Sasha, what's this about? Did something happen?"

"No, it's just that Phoenix said something today about me not knowing how to have fun."

"I wondered when that would happen."

"What do you mean?"

"Phoenix sounds like a sneaky young man."

"It's nothing like that. I mean, we were out shopping today and he called himself cheering me up by buying me some stuff. Sometimes I don't even know why he brings me along."

"Probably just likes you there because you're mature. Makes him look good, having his assistant along."

"Maybe I do need to do something, meet somebody. You know, have some fun."

"Yeah, you do that. But just make sure you're not having fun with Phoenix and be careful of accepting all those damn gifts. We both know there's gonna be a price attached."

4

THE TRIAL

November 1998

By late November I was back in Philly for the trial. Even though my attorney, Joel, tried to prepare me, I didn't know what to really expect. I did know I was scared. Daddy came to court when he could, but since he felt Paulette's family didn't have a strong case, he expected me to be alright on my own. Everyone else in the courtroom seemed connected to someone except for me. It was like a high school dance, with boys on one side and girls on the other, but this time it was Cole's family on one side and Paulette's on the other.

The hardest part about it all was having to face Cole while he was on the stand. They'd even brought his son into court the day I testified. I was glad that Daddy had come that day because his appearance gave me something from which to draw some strength. But even with my daddy in the courtroom, I nearly broke down on the stand, knowing I'd played a part in that boy losing his mother. I certainly knew what that was like and now I was carrying the guilt of his loss, too.

Cole refused to look at me and treated me like a stranger. Even though my lawyer suggested I do the same, I could feel Cole and how he'd detached himself from me. I couldn't stop my heart from aching for him, an ache I knew would never disappear.

Cole's family ignored me. Even his brother, Amir—whom we'd often double dated with—and his sister, whom I'd met several times. They both used to tell me that I was "so good for him." Now it was obvious that I was no good for anyone.

As the trial progressed, I wondered why Paulette's attorney had to keep pointing at me. I didn't want her to die. Hell, I didn't even want her to get hurt. But now even Cole looked at me as if it were my fault, as if I'd pulled the damn trigger. It was hard not to show emotion, to not let them know how much I was hurting and how much guilt I really felt. Thank God there were no jurors to stare at me. Just the judge, the lawyers, the families, and the empty chair where Paulette would've sat.

I wondered about Paulette. In my five years with Cole we'd rarely talked about her. Our relationship had never been based on his dissatisfaction with his wife. So in order to learn more about her I found myself reading the newspapers that ran stories about the trial. According to articles in the *Philadelphia Tribune* and *Philadelphia Inquirer,*

Paulette had been a devout Christian, wife, and mother. Her friends and family said they'd never even suspected there were problems in the Allen household.

"I want to give him what he's been wanting over the last five years," she'd been quoted telling one of her church sisters, who naturally assumed it was another child.

Her minister weaved a story of how she worshipped her husband and son. The only indication of trouble was her cousin testifying that she'd asked him to record phone calls between me and Cole. Of course, there were never any comments from Cole. The one thing that surprised me was that Paulette and I shared the same birthday, November third.

My mind drifted in and out of the trial. I only half-ass listened as Rankins, Stiles, and the medical examiner testified. I could hear their blanket statements. "It was established that Sasha Borianni and Cole Allen had been involved in an affair for about five years.

"According to police reports, Paulette Allen committed suicide at about 10:00 P.M. in the bedroom of her husband's mistress while they lay in bed. At approximately 10:15 P.M. police responded to a call from a frantic Ms. Borianni that someone had been shot in her home. When the police arrived, they found Ms. Allen shot through the head."

I didn't want to turn into some drunk, but I couldn't help drinking myself to sleep at night. During the day I took Xanax, and just to keep my sanity I sipped Courvoisier on ice or Heineken in between. This kept me comfortably numb so I didn't care what people said about me, or how they tried to look deep into my soul to see the part of me that was so cruel, so evil, that I could drive a person to suicide. But no matter how hard they stared, they wouldn't find that dark corner because I wasn't that person. I loved Cole and never wanted to hurt Paulette, much less cause her death.

When I wasn't drinking or in court, I busied myself with work for Phoenix. Some nights I'd find myself on the phone with him for hours, and he gradually convinced me to talk about my relationship with Cole. Phoenix even offered to come to court with me, but I told him that would be bad for his image. After talking with Phoenix one night, things got really bad when, as I was rearranging furniture in my room, I found a piece of Paulette attached to her earring under my bed. Not knowing what else to do, I took Phoenix's suggestion, left the house, and drove to D.C. where he'd just finished playing. It was totally innocent, my sleeping in the bed with him that night. He never tried to come on to me, just comforted me while I cried. Phoenix told me how he used his confidence to the point of being cocky when he needed to be and told me I needed to use that same attitude to get through my trial. I knew it wasn't a good idea to lean on him but I had to do something to stop the way my body still ached for Cole.

I thought I was prepared for whatever fate dealt me at the trial. I refused to let Joel bring in any character witnesses for me. It wasn't like I could deny my relationship with Cole. The prosecutor scrutinized every aspect of my life and I knew there was the chance that I would have to pay monetary damages, possibly even give up my house. But Paulette's family had to show by "a preponderance of the evidence" that Cole and I were liable for Paulette's death in order for that to happen. All the legal mumbo jumbo during the trial was driving me crazy.

Even though Joel wasn't billing me at the normal rate, his services were very expensive. When I tried to make payment arrangements with him, he told me my bill had been taken care of by Mr. Carter. Although I wondered about Phoenix's motives, I thanked him. He acted like it was no big deal, but I was grateful because the money Phoenix contributed allowed me top quality legal advice, which led to a verdict of not guilty. Cole was also found not guilty, but lost custody of his son to his mother-in-law.

Even though Cole and I were found not guilty, I knew deep in my heart that we were. Had it not been for our relationship—for me—Paulette would still be alive. The papers had a field day with the story. Mitchell had even been approached with the idea of a movie, which I was totally against.

I watched Cole walk out first, my eyes focused on his back and the tenseness in his shoulders. I was trying to imagine what was going on in his head and how he was feeling, having lost so much. His wife, his son, and even me. Before I could even wonder if there would ever be a way for me to reach out to him, microphones were forced in my face. Joel tried to shield me from the reporters by telling them that I had no comment, but they were insistent.

"Come on, Ms. Borianni. You need to stop hiding behind your lawyer and tell us how you feel about all this."

"Will you and Mr. Allen reunite now that the trial is over?"

"Isn't there something you want to say to the Allen family?"

I tried to squeeze back tears behind my sunglasses. I looked at them, the media who'd made a mockery week after week of my affair with Cole and his wife's death, and I knew then that there was something I needed to say. I stepped in front of the closest microphone, intent on telling everyone, especially Cole, that I was sorry. But instead I was bombarded with so many questions and camera flashes that I got confused. I wasn't sure who to answer first and when I did open my mouth to speak the only words that came out were, "You can all kiss my ass," which was repeated over and over on just about every channel.

5

CAUGHT UP

December 1999

At first I had been uneasy working so closely with Phoenix. But after a year had passed, it all seemed trivial. I put every effort into making Phoenix, and by association myself, a success. He had stuck by me through the trial and I felt I owed him. And the only way I knew how to repay him was through hard work. Over the last year our personal and business lives had become entwined, and the more time we spent together, the more I found myself attracted to him in ways that I was sure weren't healthy.

Working as his assistant was more than the executive secretary job I'd envisioned. My job was to effectively manage his activities off the court. I dealt with his public relations, marketing, and worked with the NBA league office to make sure everything in his life flowed smoothly. His image was very important to his endorsers and it was my job to leverage these relationships and ensure there were no conflicts of interest. Endorsing Nike shoes and apparel meant it was the only sporting attire he was allowed to wear, and it was often my job to lay those clothes out when he made appearances.

At first I was grateful that he was becoming dependent on me. That is, until I began to notice his subtle flirting. I tried to ignore his arm around my chair, when his fingers caressed my shoulder, when he wiped cookie crumbs from my cheek. I tried to ignore it and just tell myself that we had a close relationship, but my female instincts warned me that this young boy actually had more suaveness about him then some men I knew.

We'd spent many hours flying first class and there were times when I couldn't shut Phoenix up from talking about his dreams and the things he wanted to achieve. I was beginning to learn that his tough exterior was just a facade.

One afternoon, while coming in from Orlando, Phoenix was feeling a little beaten after a hard loss.

"You know, Sasha, basketball ain't all I want in my life."

"What is it you want, Phoenix?"

"I wanna own some shit. You know, have my own empire. Businesses, investments, so when I can't get up and down that court I can lay back on my money."

"Well, you're setting yourself up for that now."

"I mean, I got people I wanna make sure are taken care of."

Chuckling, I asked, "For instance?" thinking of the girl he'd meet in Orlando the night before.

"Naw, not like that. I don't care about them bitches. They ain't around for me if the money run out," he said, then glanced across the aisle at his posse. "They're the one's that'll be here for me."

That's when I began to understand why celebrities had entourages. It was to deal with the loneliness. It really was lonely at the top. I also knew that Phoenix kept so many people around him because he didn't want any of the women he ran with to be able to accuse him of rape. He always had an eyewitness lurking. Sometimes his bodyguard would even confront these women and ask them if they knew why he was there: so there would never be any doubt about Phoenix taking advantage of them.

But even living and working in Phoenix's glamorous life wasn't enough to lift the loneliness that sometimes gripped me with physical pain. When Phoenix would be out with his crew, I'd often have my meals in hotel rooms or in restaurants. I know people wondered why I was alone. I walked the streets in strange cities to pass the time; we were never in one place long enough for me to familiarize myself with them. Phoenix, though, picked up on this and invited me deeper into his world, probably because he saw I was still dwelling in the lost world that had belonged to Cole and me.

One evening I'd gone to a fund-raiser with Phoenix and Crystal in New York, and, the next morning, when the driver picked me up he informed me that Mr. Carter wanted me to meet him at his hotel before I took the train back to Philadelphia. When I arrived at the hotel I phoned Phoenix's room from the lobby, and he suggested I come upstairs. I naturally assumed Crystal was with him so when I got to the room and found the door slightly ajar, I called out to the both of them but got no answer.

I called out again when I heard Phoenix talking to someone. "Hey, where's everybody at?" I asked, stepping into the room.

I waited in the suite's living room and poured myself a glass of orange juice. Never did I expect to see Phoenix walk naked from the bedroom.

"Phoenix, what the hell are you doing? Where's Crystal?" I said choking on my juice.

"She left to go back to Chicago. What's wrong? You act like you ain't never seen a man naked before," he answered, a sexy grin spread across his face.

I turned my back to him, too afraid that I wouldn't be able to stop myself from staring. But in that short moment I could see that Phoenix's naked body was absolutely beautiful.

"Sasha, now you been in enough locker rooms to not be shocked at seeing me like this. Damn, I mean, I can't look all that bad."

"Well, I don't wanna be seeing your naked butt early in the morning so please get dressed," I said, realizing that this was clearly one of those times when I needed a towel to soak up my wetness.

Laughing, Phoenix went back into the bedroom and within a few moments he returned fully clothed.

"Don't you have to fly out with the team this after-noon?"

"Yeah, but I want you to make a run with me first. I mean, that's if you can handle it."

The stop he had to make was to his personal jeweler to pick up more diamonds and platinum, as if he needed anything else swinging from his neck. He kept trying to talk me into letting him purchase a pair of four-carat diamond earrings but I flat-out refused.

Next, we made a stop at Trump Tower to pick up money from someone he'd beat at poker the night before. I had no idea why I had to traipse along.

I was beginning to get the feeling that Phoenix's world wasn't going to be the safe haven I was seeking. It was too fast and there was too much to learn. The hardest part was learning not to accept Phoenix's world as my own.

Having had another increase in my salary, I began to redecorate my house. Since it was closed up most of the time because of my travel schedule, it seemed that Cole's scent, mixed with the smell of Paulette's blood, still permeated throughout. At first I thought I needed that scent, that I needed to be reminded of the pain I'd caused, so I coexisted with the lingering odor of death. Eventually, with Phoenix's encouragement, I decided I needed to move forward. The first thing I did was add fresh paint and wallpaper, then I carpeted the house throughout. I bought new furniture for my bedroom and living room, but I still wasn't able to sleep in the new bed. I even changed my style of dress. Working at the law firm, I'd mostly worn suits and dresses, but now that I worked for Phoenix, I was strictly casual. So as a treat I invited Arshell and her daughter on a shopping spree at King of Prussia Mall at my expense.

I had always been a simple woman. I liked designer clothes, but nothing that shouted a designer's name. Calvin Klein and Ellen Tracy were my favorites when I could afford them, and I usually carried a Coach bag. But Phoenix pushed me to be more daring. Once, while we were shopping in South Beach, he made me buy a pair of tight-ass Helmut Lang pants priced at $450, along with a Movado watch. He even tried to coerce me into getting a tattoo. But that I refused. I had to admit, I was beginning to like this new lifestyle and all that it had to offer. When I wasn't bold enough to spend Phoenix-type money, he'd just buy the item for me, telling me that I deserved it.

Working with Phoenix felt like I was creating an empire in just one person. It gave me a great feeling of power, and he seemed unable to resist having me at his beck and call. He played into my hands by acting helpless without me. He thought I was the strong one, but, really, we were playing off each other's strength.

But we had our disagreements too. The most interesting one was our different takes on the NBA draft. Earlier in the year I had accompanied Phoenix and Crystal to the draft because he had to do a series of interviews and provide guest commentary on the incoming class of players. Their ages ranged from barely eighteen to twenty-three years old. While returning from the draft in Charlotte, I made the mistake of mentioning to him that I thought draft day reminded me of the slave auction block.

"What the hell are you talking about, Sasha?"

"Look at it like this, Phoenix. These brothers wait in the 'green room' for their names to be called, hopefully in the first round if they've had the luck of being invited. Their prayer is to go to the best team, in the best market for endorsement. And, most important, the highest bidder. Then their name is called and they don the hat of the winning team, kiss their family and friends good-bye, hug their more-than-likely Jewish agent, and walk up on the podium, aka auction block, to say hello, smile, and shake hands with the headmaster, better known as the 'commissioner.' From then on, Phoenix, you belong to them and they can ship you anywhere they want."

"Get the fuck outta here, Sasha! Don't nobody own me or tell me what to do."

Even Crystal chimed in, "So, Phoenix, you don't think you could be traded?"

"Fuck no. My team needs me. Shit, I am the team!"

I could tell my comparison was bothering him but I was on a roll and wanted to prove my point. What the hell did he know anyway?

"Phoenix, if your 'owner,' Mr. I-ain't-a-slave-holder thought there was somebody better than you, you'd be uprooted and couldn't really say a word."

"Ain't no way they'd do that shit. Not to Phoenix Carter. Anyway, you think I care? As much money as I'm getting?"

"Yeah, you care, or otherwise we wouldn't be having this conversation. You and I both know there is no loyalty in professional sports. And let's not even talk about the role these shoe companies play, OK?"

"Check this shit out. If these pilgrims wanna give me millions to run up and down that hardwood then I'm taking it. Shit, they ain't nothing but a bunch of control freaks anyway. What else they gonna do with that money?"

"OK. So then let's just say that some of us are getting our reparations," I answered.

We cut the conversation short because I could tell by the number of drinks we were ordering and the stares from the other first-class passengers that the conversation had more truth to it than any of us were willing to admit.

But the more I thought about it the more I realized just how entwined politics, sports, and entertainment were. Yeah, I was learning a lot, but so too was Phoenix Carter.

Right after Christmas, Chicago had three consecutive home games so I decided to hang out in Chicago with Phoenix and get some work done. He'd sent his body-guard, Trey, to O'Hare airport to pick me up. Trey must have weighed over 300 pounds and stood about six foot five inches tall. My first night in town, rather than go to the Four Seasons and check in, we went directly to the game then out to dinner afterward at Charlie Trotter's with Phoenix, his entourage, and a few teammates. You never had to order when you were dining with Phoenix because he usually ordered damn near everything on the menu and just passed it around. He was in a good mood, as they'd just beat Philly by ten points, which broke their three-game losing streak. Phoenix was celebrating with plenty of Cristal. Being with them was always easy and I actually had a good time laughing and talking about the crazy world they lived in, the one I slipped in and out of. Everyone always had so many stories to tell about fans, groupies, and money-hungry family members. When the conversation turned to sex, as it usually did at a table full of young men, I should've paid more attention when Phoenix's eyes lingered on me too long, and when his leg brushed against mine and stayed there.

Since Phoenix and Trey had been drinking, I chauf-feured us back to the house in his Range Rover. Phoenix suggested I stay in the guest room so I wouldn't have to go back to the city. His home was an estate in the promi-nent community of Deerfield, Illinois, located on the out-skirts of Chicago.

Arriving at the black wrought-iron gates of Phoenix's estate, I noticed the property looked dark, with the exception of the soft lighting surrounding his house that came on automatically at dusk. I asked him where Crystal and the children were and he responded that they were attending a funeral in Atlanta. Crystal rarely missed a home game, as she not only wanted to support him but this was, I'm sure, her way of keeping a watchful eye on her sought-after husband. I wondered, though, how much of an eye she really kept on him, since Phoenix always did whatever he wanted.

We entered the house through the six-car garage where he kept his two Range Rovers, Ferrari, Bentley, and Benz. Once inside, Trey went to the guesthouse that was attached by an enclosed walkway to the main house, and I went to put my bags away in one of the bedrooms upstairs.

Phoenix decided he wanted to soak in the Jacuzzi, which was situated in the pool house. I'd always liked this part of the house because of its large indoor trees, bamboo furnishings, and retractable ceiling. I'd never used the facilities though Crystal and Phoenix often invited me to do so.

Phoenix suggested I keep him company, which usually meant me sitting in a chair and updating him on his schedule and the various requests for his appearance. I hadn't drunk much during dinner, so I decided to indulge by pouring us snifters of Hennessy, or "Hen-Dog," as Phoenix called it. He started the water for the Jacuzzi, turned his stereo on with Jay-Z singing "Big Pimpin'," and tuned the large flat-screen television to *SportsCenter.* He then took a quick shower and returned with a large white cotton Polo towel wrapped around him.

I'd thought he'd at least have on swimming trunks, so I tried not to act like it was a big deal when he pulled the towel off, exposed his naked body, and stepped into the water. I tried to look at him like the young man he was, but I couldn't stop myself from looking a little longer at his long, lean, and muscular body. The one thing Phoenix was truly faithful to was his rigorous workout schedule. He worked out three times a week, for two and a half hours a day, in addition to practice with the team. His body showed it and any woman who watched basketball knew Phoenix had the best arms in the league. His body could seduce any woman, especially me.

As I stretched out in the chaise lounge, I couldn't help but notice from the corner of my eye that his long dick was quite hard as he slid into the water. While he concentrated on getting the water temperature right, I took a moment to steal a glance at him, and wondered what it would be like to have his young body close against mine. Once his body was covered with bubbles I felt safe to begin our conversation.

"I finally secured meetings with American Express and Pepsi. They'd both like to bring you up to their corporate offices so we can seal the endorsement deal."

He sipped on his drink and said, "I knew you'd make it happen. What else you got?"

"I've been checking the votes for the All-Star Team and you're still leading all players. But I'm sure you already knew that."

"Got it," he said before splashing water on his face.

"It's still early but I've already started getting requests to book you for some summer events. You also have a commercial shoot with Nike that's set for next week while you're playing in Portland."

"Talk about that summer shit to Crystal. I think she wants to take a few vacations next year."

I continued on about two magazines that were offering to do cover stories on him, but I could tell by the look on his face and the way he was pulling on his dick under the water that he was totally disinterested in my talk of business. Instead of answering my questions, he just sipped on his drink and watched me like he wanted me.

"Come on. Why don't you get in with me?" he said, nodding toward the steaming water.

"Please, Phoenix, stop playing. You're drunk."

"Come on, when's the last time—"

"What I do is none of your business, especially who I sleep with."

Phoenix knew I wasn't seeing anyone. He made sure that if I did, it wasn't anybody he knew. Months ago, when one of the Nike executives had started asking about me, Phoenix had rudely told him that I was off-limits. I acted as if he was just trying to protect me, but when I told Arshell, she warned me to be careful because it sounded like he was saving me for himself.

"So you getting in or what?" he asked as he dipped in and out of the steamy water.

I had to admit I was tempted. In an effort to redirect my thoughts, I stood up and walked over to the floor-to-ceiling windows that overlooked the grounds, trying to reason with myself that it wasn't even right for me to be considering this. I tried to concentrate on the snow that had been falling hard since I'd arrived in Chicago, but standing there looking through the frosted window I felt my insides heating up, so I poured myself another drink.

"What's wrong, Sasha Borianni? You scared of a young boy?"

"Have I ever appeared scared of anything?"

"Well, then, strip that shit off and get in."

I crossed the room and stood against the wall, looking at him. It was clear that he was baiting me. He made it look so damn tempting as he slid in and out of the water, bubbles all over his head. Even with all his millions and his body decorated with tattoos, he was still a kid taking a bubble bath. But this kid was asking a woman old enough to be his mother to join him. By now, though, he wasn't asking with words. He was taunting me with his eyes.

"When's the last time you relaxed in some bubbles?"

"Phoenix, I know how to relax," I said, my voice shaking.

"What if I promise you I won't even come over to your side of the Jacuzzi?"

"I don't know, Phoenix. I mean, what if—"

"Damn, Sash, C'mon, bring those long legs over here."

"OK, alright. I'll get in, but I'm not getting naked," I said even though I knew it sounded stupid.

Laughing, he watched me with those sleepy eyes of his and told me to bring him the bottle of "Hen-Dog." Standing close to where he sat, he looked up at me as I slid out of my tights and stepped out of my wool skirt. I pulled my sweater over my head slowly, 'cause I could see my undressing was turning him on. I stepped into the hot water wearing a pair of white low-rider bikinis and matching bra, hardly believing what I was doing. While I sat at one corner and him at the other we both broke out in laughter because it was funny. It had to be; otherwise I couldn't have done it. To try to contain my nervousness, I poured myself a full snifter of Hennessy and drank it straight down. My insides were on fire not only from the Hennessy, but because it had been so long since I'd been with a man.

Phoenix, on the other hand, had a lot of women, young, firm bodies that mine couldn't match. I'd seen him with women who looked like they walked off the pages of a magazine and girls who were bred for music videos. Even though I knew my body wasn't lacking, I was still embarrassed for him to see me naked. He didn't seem to mind, and wasted no time in wrapping his long hard legs around my thighs and pulling at my bra straps. I didn't resist, so he unhooked my bra and tossed it across the marble tiled floor. My breasts weren't big, but they were still full and firm. At seeing them he licked his lips.

"Damn, Sasha, your shit look good."

I began to accept the fact that there was no way out of this. I'd helped to create this situation so I just had to be a woman and deal with it. I said nothing as he eased my panties down and let them float in the water. I felt myself really want him, and that's when he didn't look like a boy anymore. Rather than look at him, I closed my eyes and enjoyed the sensation of his tongue gently licking my nipples, one at a time, until both were hard enough to burst.

"See, it's not that bad. I promise you're gonna like it," he said, then he kissed me. His tongue felt so good moving into the grooves of my mouth that I gave in to him. I knew I was crossing into a realm from which I could never return, but at the same time I couldn't stop. I felt the hot liquor coursing through my body, and suddenly all my resistance slipped away.

Phoenix trailed kisses along my jaw and I was finally able to catch my breath. Then, in one swift move, he sat me on top of him and pushed himself inside me with a force that made me gasp. We both stared at each other without saying anything while our bodies began to slowly move until I stopped because it was too much for me. But he wouldn't let go; he pressed his lips against mine with a passion I hadn't felt since I'd been with Cole. Phoenix pulled himself from inside me, stood up and led me out of the water. I was completely in his spell.

He situated me on the chaise lounge, in a position where he could easily enter me. But before he did that, he stretched my legs apart, straddling them on top of his shoulders and knelt down in front of me and tasted the juices that I'd been holding in since I'd felt this situation unfolding. I tried to reason with myself, maybe justify what was happening, but the way he was enjoying the taste of me, all I could say was, "Oh shit!"

The next thing I knew, he was standing up and pulling me toward him. We kissed again and this time he gently pushed my head toward his hard dick, which was standing at attention. There was no protest from me as I moved down between his legs and took him in my mouth. As I tasted a trickle of cum seeping from him, he withdrew from me. I looked up and saw him pull a condom from underneath the chaise lounge I'd been sitting in earlier. Had he planned this, I wondered? Impossible, because there was no way he could've known I would give in to him. I tried to hesitate but he pushed me back onto the chaise and plunged himself inside me. I could hear the thumping beat of DMX shouting into my head, *"What these bitches want from a nigga?"* Nothing, nothing, I answered silently—I wanted nothing but what he was giving me right now. Phoenix pounded the walls inside me, and my head was spinning as I tried to push him farther and farther inside. This time, when we looked into each other's eyes, there was no laughter. We moved and we stroked and I felt myself caught between a dream and reality. I couldn't believe that after a year of knowing him—this boy, more than fifteen years my junior, my employer no less—that I had given myself to him so easily, but before I could finish my thoughts . . . he uttered my name and burst inside me.

6

ALL-STAR

February 2000

Nothing noticeably changed between us after that. We worked together as if we had never been together. As if he'd never been inside me or like I'd never tasted him. I couldn't talk about it anyway because that would've made it too much of a reality. I think maybe it was as taboo for him as it was for me.

Of course, the only person I could tell was Arshell. I hesitated at first, knowing she'd be pissed at me but I was actually hoping her voice of reason would make me back off. But like any good friend I also knew she would listen and at least try to understand. I phoned her one Sunday evening.

"Arshell, you busy? It's Sasha."

"No, no. I'm fixing dinner. What's going on? I left you a message a few days ago. Hold on a minute."

I heard her yelling at the kids to be quiet and then asking Wayne, her husband, to watch the food while she went upstairs.

"OK, talk. What's wrong?"

"It's Phoenix. I mean, it's me. We . . ."

"Awww shit, Sasha. Please don't tell me. Please don't tell me you slept with that boy. Why Sasha? Why did you do it? I mean, what did he offer you?"

"I didn't mean to. It was just that I needed somebody. I needed him."

"You didn't need that boy. He can't do anything for you."

I remained silent.

"I'm sorry, Sasha, but it's the truth. I mean, think about it. Haven't you had enough drama? You don't need to be starting this shit again."

"I know, but—"

"But nothing! I don't care how many times it happened, you have to stop this stupid shit right now. Quit if you have to."

"It's not that easy, Arshell."

"Sasha, he's a damn kid."

"That's where you're wrong."

"So you're gonna tell me that this boy is so good that you can't stop screwing him? C'mon, now, be for real."

"I know you're right but I swear to you nobody is gonna find out this time."

"Yeah, right. This could be a disaster for both of you and you know it. Imagine if the media got a hold of this. And what about his family."

"Damn it, you think I don't know that? But he makes it so hard for me to resist him. C'mon, you've seen him. Are you going to sit there and tell me that all those sports you watch with Wayne that you never once imagined sleeping with one of those brothers?"

"Alright, alright. So maybe he is a sexy young thing, but it can't be that good. I'm going to give you a chance to tell me how all this happened before I drive up to Philly and whip your tail. And don't leave out any dirty details."

Arshell could easily go from acting like a mother to being a raunchy girlfriend. Even though Arshell lost her virginity before me, I felt I was more experienced because of my entrance into the world of intimacy.

Our friendship had begun in high school after I'd found myself hurting over the first woman I looked up to. Maria had been an assistant teacher in my English class. She was a twenty-two-year-old Italian girl who took an interest in me after I'd spent time with her on special projects. I immediately took to her too and we became friends. One Saturday I ran into her while shopping at Wanamaker's on 13th and Market Streets. She offered to buy me lunch and took me to Kelly's Seafood. We mostly talked about school, with her trying to convince me to attend college after graduation. Before long the conversation turned to boys.

Maria was adamant that I always make myself hard to get, that boys never wanted a girl that gave it up too easy. But I think the thing that stuck with me the most was Maria's advice that I'd have to learn how to satisfy myself before I could ever tell a boy or a man what pleased me.

The next Saturday I called her and we met on South

Street to do some shopping. Afterward she offered to fix me lunch at her house. Her little row home was nice and I could tell she had more money than she made as a teacher's assistant. I helped her prepare a salad, and she reheated leftover lasagna. She was surprised that I knew what ingredients she used and I told her about my having some Italian blood. Maria then wanted to know about my mother, but I wasn't comfortable enough to talk about that yet.

After lunch, Maria opened a bottle of wine and told me about her boyfriend, Nicki, who was also Italian and owned a pizza restaurant that sold more than pizza. Nicki also sold women, at a very high price, whom he kept housed in apartments around Rittenhouse Square.

The more wine I drank, the more questions I asked about sex. I wanted to know why my friends always said it hurt yet claimed it felt good. Then there was the question of what purpose the clitoris served. She answered my questions and in turn wanted to know how far I'd actually gone with a boy. I confessed to having done no more than giving my current boyfriend a hand job until he came. She laughed at this, as she couldn't believe I hadn't yet performed oral sex. I told her that Black girls didn't do that. I also told her I hadn't gone all the way because my father hadn't yet allowed me to get on any type of birth control.

Maria then excused herself to go to the bathroom, and I walked into the living room to pour more wine. When she returned she looked at me and said, "Sasha, you know you can always learn how to satisfy a man, but first you have to learn to satisfy yourself."

Now, I'd never been a timid girl but I was a little nervous. I certainly had never masturbated. I was well aware that touching myself in certain places made me shiver but I always stopped before it felt too good. Maria must've sensed that I was curious, because she asked me if I wanted her to show me what to do. I nodded my head yes. Maria laughed and said, "Don't be so nervous." How could I not? Hell, I was sixteen and about to be seduced by a grown woman. She moved to stand so close to me that I felt her breasts touch mine. I'd never been this close to another woman and definitely never this close to a white person. She didn't kiss me, just reached for my glass of wine, took a sip and then held it to my lips. I drained it.

Maria gently tilted my head, kissing me on the neck. No boy had ever done that and I felt myself want her to hurry up and teach me everything she knew. But Maria wanted to move slowly. Once she realized that I had placed my hand on one of her breasts she smiled and softly told me how good she was going to make me feel. I wanted that feeling. She brushed her lips against mine and kissed me without opening her mouth, then moved away. She laughed, then held my chin and kissed me deep and slow, far better than a boy had ever kissed me.

When she stopped kissing me I felt dizzy from either her kiss or the wine. I stumbled a little before gaining my balance and she asked me if I was okay. I nodded yes. She then suggested we sit down and led me to the couch. Sitting there with my hands tucked under my thighs I watched her undress.

"Sasha, have you ever seen a woman naked?" she asked, then proceeded to pull her tight-fitting sundress over her head, exposing her panties and bra.

"Not really," I answered, staring at her. Maria had a body like the women I saw on television. Her breasts bulged out of her bra and she had a little ass, which was barely covered with what she called a G-string.

I was wearing shorts and a tube top, which she easily removed. When she was finished I stood naked in front of her and no part of me was embarrassed.

She said, "Everything I do to you I want you to tell me how it feels." She pulled me to her and kissed me again but this time she had one hand on my ass and the other on my breasts, gently gliding her hands over me. She moved her mouth to my neck and bit all around it. I jumped at the feeling and told her it tickled. "Good," she said.

Next she took both my breasts in her hands and told me that a man should always treat my breasts with care. She began fondling them, licking my nipples and squeezing them just enough to give me pleasure. I couldn't believe I could feel this good and still be a virgin. My breathing was heavy but I was no longer nervous.

"Take my bra off, Sasha," she said.

I pulled the straps of her bra down, turned her around, and unsnapped it. Then she turned and told me to take off her G-string. I pulled it down, she stepped out of it, and I noticed she barely had hair covering her. I had an entire Afro. She saw my surprise and told me she'd also teach me how to shave. Now that we were both naked, she took me by the hand and led me to the couch. I sat on the edge of the cushion.

Kneeling in front of me she placed her hands on my knees and pulled my legs apart. "Remember," she said, "tell me what feels good." At this she eased her head between my legs and entered me with her tongue. My first reaction was to scream, so I covered my mouth and responded by arching my back, giving her more of me. Maria's tongue roamed the parts of me that were supposed to be private. I was unable to talk until she pulled her head away and told me, "You're not talking to me, Sasha."

"OK," I managed to murmur but couldn't imagine that words existed for the sensations her tongue created. When she again planted herself inside me, I was half off the couch and began talking to her as I gyrated my pelvis against her mouth.

"Maria, that feels so good." She started to slow down until I begged her, "Please, please don't stop."

She pulled her head away and asked, "Now, who else has made you feel like this, Sasha?"

"Nobody, Maria. Nobody but you."

With that she stuck her finger inside me and took my clitoris between her lips. I screamed out as I felt a rush through my entire body and a thick liquid oozing from me. After lingering between my legs, she stood up and said, "Now see, Sasha. You just had your first orgasm and you're still a virgin."

Over the course of the school year my relationship with Maria flourished and I began to look up to her. Each time I visited she made sure a river flowed from me. But never once would she let me do more than suck her breasts because, as she reminded me, I was not a lesbian. She just seemed to get so much pleasure from pleasing me. Never once did I feel guilty and I damn sure didn't share my experience with anyone. Maria made sure I'd return each week by promising me gifts. There was lingerie from stores I'd never heard of, clothes from boutiques, expensive pocketbooks and makeup, which was to enhance my beauty, she told me. But mostly I liked the things she told me about how to satisfy a man. There were other things too, like teaching me to shop at the Reading Terminal and cook like a real Italian. She awakened my taste buds with various cheeses, spices, garlic, and multicolor peppers and onions. I enjoyed it all while Maria teased me, "Sasha, maybe you're more Italian than you care to admit."

But our friendship didn't last long because Nicki didn't like my being around. While visiting one Saturday I overheard Maria in tears trying to explain our relationship to him. When he began slapping her I screamed to call the police. But Maria didn't want my help and cruelly told me to get out. It was at that moment I knew I wouldn't be seeing her anymore.

It was Arshell who found me crying in a darkened classroom and listened to my admission of shame. For what would be the first time of many, she reassured me that it wasn't my fault. Rather than accuse me of being a lesbian, Arshell told me that Maria was just someone I was supposed to meet. But she also surprised me by wanting to know the details of exactly what I'd done with Maria. Thus began my friendship with Arshell and her living vicariously through me. How could I have known that I would continue to provide enough excitement for the both of us?

By now I'd proven myself to be invaluable to Phoenix. A cell phone and PDA made me accessible to him twenty-four hours a day, and that's how he liked it. He no longer needed his memory; he relied on me to know what he needed and to be prepared for wherever he had to go, whether it be professional or personal. The only thing that made it easier was that during the season—November to June—his distractions were less, as all his time was devoted to basketball. I rarely needed to travel with the team except when he had appearances in those cities. Nevertheless, he always found a reason for me to come along, especially when Crystal wasn't there.

Phoenix and I could not keep our hands off each other. I never even noticed who would initiate it. All I knew was that I had to have Phoenix Carter and it seemed he had to have me.

On the business front, I had begun to gather information on setting up his charitable foundation and already had donors. Along with Mitchell, we'd been interviewing for a director for his organization. I actually wanted to assume that position, but Phoenix didn't want me in an office; he wanted me around him as much as possible. As part of his charitable work, Phoenix insisted that he participate in ten charity events a year that didn't include any publicity. He'd also begun to hire staff for Carter Enterprises, which had now grown to seventy employees. Their primary business was managing Phoenix's assets and endorsements, while I now focused on his public image.

Since I'd come on board, his image had taken a turn for the better. In addition to his lucrative sneaker deal, he was the youngest NBA athlete to get an endorsement with Mercedes-Benz (for their new line of two-seater drop tops). There was also the possibility of him endorsing Timberland, a deal I'd gone after, and practically sealed, without him even being aware. Even though people still thought he was an arrogant thug, they couldn't ignore him because he was the league's leading scorer and the NBA's most sought-after player.

By February, the NBA was about to break for All-Star weekend. Chicago was in their last game against New York at the Garden. I was in the media room, jockeying reporters who wanted exclusive postgame interviews. From the television monitor I could see Chicago would win, which meant Phoenix would be in a good mood. Ever since Phoenix had been voted onto the All-Star team I couldn't keep up with the many requests that had poured in, and tonight was no different. I had even been considering hiring my own assistant. The next afternoon we were flying to San Antonio for the All-Star game, where he'd meet Crystal, the kids, and his parents, so I had to squeeze in as many interviews as possible after tonight's game. I was glad I'd also invited my son, Owen, and his wife, Deirdre, to join us in San Antonio.

Once Phoenix's interviews finished at the Garden, we had dinner at Moomba and then went to his brownstone in Brooklyn. Knowing I'd be up late making changes to his itinerary, I showered, put on sweats, and settled into his office to rework his schedule. I needed to have a minute-by-minute itinerary for Nike, the NBA, Crystal, and Trey. I'd learned in this business that nothing was ever confirmed until it actually happened. You had to be prepared for anything. By now Phoenix was no longer tardy for appointments and actually kept the majority of them. Every minute of his time had to be accounted for. It was a big undertaking, as he needed to be accounted for during periods when he really would be unavailable. Knowing Phoenix, when he didn't have business obligations he'd be spending that time with another woman, or simply locked up in a hotel room gambling. I was sure he and his All-Star teammates had private parties planned every night. Thank God I didn't have to be involved in setting those up. One thing I did know was that Phoenix was good for buying and using condoms.

Phoenix had decided not to go out this evening and was upstairs watching a tape of the game he'd just played. Everyone else was out for the night. About 2:00 A.M., just as I was wrapping up, Phoenix came into the office and asked me if I wanted to watch a movie.

We went into his viewing room on the top floor of the brownstone. It was furnished with an overstuffed sofa, two recliners, and a 60-inch television screen. We sat in separate recliners, watching *Dead Presidents,* for the umpteenth time. I enjoyed being with him like this, when he was in his boxers and tee shirt. It made me want to treat him like a little boy and take care of him, especially when he complained about his aching body. So when he asked me if I would give him a massage, before I could think about it, I found myself agreeing. He could see in my eyes, though, that I was questioning what we were about to do next. And before I could change my mind, he led me by the hand from the room. As we walked the short distance down the hallway toward the gym I tried to tell myself that this would be the last time. I tried not to focus on the muscles in his back, so I took in the glass cabinet that lined one side of the hall. The cabinet encased his many trophies, and on the other wall were photos of him and various celebrities. But my attempt to distract myself was futile. I knew what waited for me in the room with Phoenix and I was looking forward to it. There was no denying that Arshell had been right—I was getting hooked on Phoenix, and if I kept at it I'd never look anywhere else for love. But how could I, or any woman, ever resist a man so sexy and so willing to go to any length to satisfy a woman?

Once in the gym we didn't even talk. I went to the cabinet and retrieved the oils his trainer used as he undressed and climbed onto the massage table. I felt myself wanting to stop what I was doing but a greater part of me couldn't resist. So I went to his stretched out body, oiled my hands with the vanilla and sandalwood blend and pressed my palms into his back. Before long I found myself without thoughts as I enjoyed the total surrender of him. It was clear from the low moaning he made when I touched a part of him that was more tender than others that he was enjoying it, too. From his back to his chest, his body was both smooth and rough. I couldn't seem to massage hard enough.

I could feel the knots releasing in his muscles as spasms passed through him. I poured all of me into relaxing him. I wanted him to feel me under his skin, so I continued with soothing strokes, working his entire body, relieving muscle tension and loosening his sore joints.

He tried to talk to me, but I didn't want our voices to interrupt the peaceful quiet of the house, so I shushed him. As my hands traveled across his slightly hairy chest, I noticed that I'd massaged him into a hardness that looked painful. The moment was too good to waste and Phoenix, recognizing this, whined to me like the little boy he was. "C'mon, Sasha. Please let me put this in you." But I wouldn't stop. Instead I began to kiss the places that I'd massaged until I reached his hardness. I took him into my mouth and allowed him to roam the warmth under and around my tongue. As his body moved closer to the edge of the table, I realized Phoenix was no longer in control and I loved it. Loved him holding on to my head, begging me not to stop . . . and letting himself go, his sperm filling my mouth until his body weakly collapsed on the table. I rested my head on his stomach until I heard his breathing slow down and knew he was asleep.

Hours later, arriving in San Antonio, I became panic-stricken at the thought of having to see Crystal. I mean, this wasn't like it had been with Paulette. I knew Crystal, her family, and her children. Worse, I'd listened to her cry about Phoenix and the other women she'd found out about. How could I face her knowing I was one of those very women she despised? Maybe it wasn't too late. Maybe I could still back out of this affair with her man—too young to even be a man—who moved me in all the wrong ways.

Who was I fooling? We were just getting started.

The frenzy of All-Star weekend left me with little free time. The weekend was filled with limo rides from venue to venue. I was being pulled in so many directions I didn't have time to dwell on the awkwardness I felt being around Crystal. My son and his wife were on their own and didn't seem to mind, as I'd made sure they had tickets to all the events. That's how it was All-Star weekend. Money could buy anything—tickets at astronomical prices, betting, gambling, and prostitution were part of the foundation. It was a challenge just getting in and out of the hotel lobby. Fans, athletes, entertainers, and reporters covered the city of San Antonio. It didn't help that I was premenstrual and fighting with a headache and cramps. I had made such a name for myself working for Phoenix that I was even approached by other athletes with job opportunities. I knew, though, that Phoenix was too selfish for me to entertain the idea of taking on additional work, or even meeting with men socially. One evening I went out to dinner with a very prominent agent, a white man, who was known around the league for his interest in Black women, and me in particular. Later that night, while sharing a cognac with him in an intimate corner of the hotel lobby, I noticed Phoenix and his entourage walking toward the elevators. He played it cool but couldn't resist making his way over to us.

"Yo, Sash. What's up?"

The agent stood up to greet Phoenix. "Hey, Phoenix. Man, how's it going?"

Phoenix barely shook his extended hand but kept his eyes on me. I was hoping the agent didn't notice.

"I'm cool. What's up with you, Sasha?"

"Nothing, just relaxing. Where's the entourage going tonight?" I asked, looking up at him.

"Everybody's chilling. We got an early start tomorrow. Isn't that what you told me?"

"Sure did. I guess you better go get some rest."

"Yeah, alright," he said, then abruptly walked away.

Later that night, after having gone to my room, Phoenix knocked on the door.

Cracking the door open, I said, "What are you doing here? How do you know I don't have company?"

"Bullshit. Open the door, Sasha," he said, pushing past me and looking around the room.

It was apparent to me what he'd really come for was reassurance that I was still for his enjoyment alone.

"Damn, you can't just bust in here, you know."

"So, what's up? You doing pilgrims now?" he asked, while he lay across my bed and lit up a joint. He didn't smoke often but I guess he considered this his time off.

"I believe I can do whoever I want," I answered, while standing against the closed door.

"Not while you're working for me you can't," he said. "Come on over here, girl, and sit down. You want some?" he asked pointing the joint in my direction.

I sat on the foot of the bed and took a few puffs. "Seriously, though, you were the one who told me I needed to have some fun."

"We gonna have some fun tonight, ain't we?"

"This is not a good night. It's that time of the month for me."

Phoenix rubbed his fingers across my lips. "So does that mean it's not a good time of the month for me too?"

Even with his wife and family on another floor in the hotel I knew there was no getting rid of him without satisfying him first. After making him beg and plead, I agreed to go down on him until he'd exhausted himself. Afterward, as I watched him sleep, I vowed this would be the last time I'd taste Phoenix Carter's cum.

Little did I know that two weeks later he'd give me a diamond and platinum tennis bracelet, "for all your hard-ass work" he'd said. The diamonds weren't as big as the ones in Crystal's bracelet, but they were still bigger than what I would've been able to afford. He wanted me to wear it every day, but I only wore it on special occasions, like the Essence Awards that I attended with Crystal and Arshell, and the ESPYs that we attended with Phoenix's entourage. Of course, he won Athlete of the Year.

But jewelry wasn't the only gift I received from Phoenix.

One morning when I was leaving to fly to Chicago my

phone rang. It was the Wilke Lexus dealer of Ardmore, wanting to know if I would be available to accept the delivery of my new truck. I told the salesman I knew nothing about a delivery, but he informed me that Phoenix Carter had ordered me a new 2000 Lexus, which would be arriving at my door shortly. When the doorbell rang a few minutes later, I walked outside and there, in my driveway, sat a pearl-colored Lexus LX 450 with chocolate brown Coach leather interior. Maybe sleeping with him had been worth it. Hell, a new truck with no payments—what could be wrong with that? Now we were both getting perks. When I called to thank Phoenix, he laughed and said, "Yo, that's the shit you should be driving, working for me. Not no damn Honda Accord."

7

GOLDEN BOY

July 2000

Basketball season was finally over. Chicago had made it to the semifinals but fell short of beating Philly by three points, which made me secretly happy. During the off-season Phoenix usually took vacation during July and then in August and September he began to do celebrity appearances, basketball camps, and commercial shoots. I was glad for the chance to get away from the madness of our personal and business relationship, even though for the most part, I thought I juggled it well. I justified it by telling myself that what I was doing wasn't so wrong. I mean, I'd done it before with other lovers but I somehow convinced myself that this time it wasn't the same because I wasn't in love with Phoenix.

For July Fourth weekend Arshell and her husband were having their yearly barbeque, which I never missed. I drove down to their home in Maryland two days early just so I could spend time with my best friend before everybody arrived.

Arshell had a beautiful single home situated in Burtonsville. She no longer worked full time as a pharmacist but stayed at home raising her three children and going to school for yet another degree. Her husband, Wayne R. Wayne—why his parents named him that beats the hell outta me—was a computer analyst at IBM. He was always after me to meet one of his coworkers, but promised that he'd have no blind dates for me this weekend. I often envied Arshell and her happy family life. I knew it wasn't in the plans for me. Maybe before Cole there might've been a chance for me to meet a nice guy, but all that died along with Paulette.

The day before the 'que, the house was in a frenzy, so I took the children to the pool. Arshell had a fifteen-year-old daughter and a set of three-year-old twin boys. When we returned to the house, while the kids were upstairs changing, I sat in the kitchen drinking water and eating grapes, never expecting that someone was about to enter my life. Then, in the back door comes this brother about six foot three inches tall, golden brown, muscular and fine, claiming to be a friend of Wayne R. Wayne. Impossible!

"Well, you must be a new friend, 'cause I never met you before," I said as he walked in.

"Actually, I'm an old friend. You are?" he asked, almost sarcastically.

"Oh, my name is Sasha," I answered.

"I've never heard of you either," he replied, while lifting a case of sodas onto the kitchen counter, all the while taking in my long legs.

"And your name is?" I inquired, looking at the muscles in his back contracting.

"Trent Russell. Well, Ms. Sasha, from the looks of that body, maybe you could help me with these bags."

I began helping him put groceries away. But before we could engage in any further conversation Arshell and Wayne arrived at the house. I immediately pulled her into the living room to get some details on this hunk of a man.

"Who the hell is that in your kitchen?" I asked, pulling on her arm.

"That's Trent. Wayne's li'l childhood buddy."

"That much I know, but who is he and why's he here?"

"Girl, you're crazy. He grew up with Wayne and this is the first opportunity they've had to get together in years."

"Where's he staying? Did he come with anyone?"

"Damn, Sasha, I haven't seen you this excited about a man since you met Phoenix."

"Don't start with that. I told you I'm ending it with him. Now, give me the scoop."

"He's staying down at the Crowne Plaza, and as for his availability, you'll have to ask him."

The next day Trent and I still hadn't had a chance to talk because the house was full of people. The men wanted to talk basketball with me and women were competing for Trent's attention. I always found it interesting that I seemed to be a magnet to unavailable men and wondered what about me said I was available.

Eventually Trent caught my eye and he nodded his

head for me to meet him in the house. I excused myself and went inside. "Let's take a walk," he suggested. I couldn't have been happier to agree. I did most of the talking as we walked behind Arshell's housing development and onto a bike trail. Trent had a way of asking me questions without talking much about himself. I could tell he was a quiet man, and it was something about that quietness that attracted me. He never asked me about my past or present relationships, nor did I ask him. From the tone of our conversation I assumed that Wayne R. Wayne hadn't planned this encounter.

"Tell me about yourself. What do you do up there in Philly?"

"Actually, I'm not there too often. My job causes me to travel a lot."

"And what do you do?"

"I'm an assistant for Phoenix Carter," I said, watching him closely to gauge his reaction.

"Not a bad job, I guess. What do you do as his assistant?"

I was tongue-tied, momentarily thinking of the things I'd done for Phoenix lately.

"A little bit of everything, I guess you could say. From PR to juggling his schedule."

"And what else do you do?"

I wanted to lie and say I had a life, that I went out with friends, took vacations. Instead I changed the subject and told him about my plans for the upcoming week.

"Actually, I'm driving back to Philly tomorrow. From there I'm flying to L.A. to spend a week with my son and his family. Then I'm back into BWI to watch Arshell and Wayne's gang for four days so they can get away."

"I see. How's this? Why don't I drop you off in Philly on my way home? That way we can get to know each other a little better. Your car will be waiting here when you return to babysit."

After spending the morning putting Arshell and Wayne's house back in order, the following evening we hit I-95 for Philly in Trent's black '99 Ford Expedition. We didn't talk much, just listened to the various CDs he had. Trent made me laugh deep, hearty laughs, and I wasn't even sure what I was laughing about. He wasn't at all impressed by my job and for that I was grateful. Football was his favorite sport, and the Giants were at the head of his list of favorite teams. We teased each other and made bets, Eagles vs. Giants for the upcoming season. During the ride I found out that Trent was a thirty-eight-year-old electrician for a private utility company and resided in Short Hills, New Jersey. He'd never married, but did have a thirteen-year-old daughter, Briana, who lived with her mother. He was very knowledgeable about politics and hoped to run for office one day, and wanted to start his political career by running for president of the local union. Trent told me stories about his job that I found fascinating. Early in his career he'd had a lot of close calls with being electrocuted. Now, though, as local union representative, his position was mostly administrative. He taught classes at Seton Hall, his alma mater, where he'd majored in political science. He sat on the board of the Joint Apprentice Training Committee, was a member of the Electrical Code Examination Board, and he'd been recognized on numerous occasions for outstanding work and was aligning himself with the right people to be ready when election time came. But he always kept his hands in the "heat," as he called it. And I could certainly feel the heat rising between us, though neither of us mentioned it.

"So, why the two professions? Being an electrician and politician don't exactly go together."

"Yeah, that's what my parents thought. When I told them I wanted to be a politician they made sure I followed in my father's footsteps of being an electrician so I'd be able to eat."

"Makes sense. I guess you know what you're doing because it's working for you."

Briefly he took his eyes off the road and glanced at me.

"I have to ask this. Is there anybody waiting for you at home?"

Before I could answer him my cell phone rang. It was Daddy checking in on me. I talked to him briefly and promised that I'd spend time with him when I got back to Philly. Then there was a call from Owen asking about my arrival time and a call from Phoenix that I cut short by telling him I was in a meeting. I never answered Trent's question.

When we arrived at my home in Chestnut Hill two hours later, it was only natural for me to invite Trent inside, something I hadn't done with a man since Cole. Though I'd only known Trent for two days, I wanted to hold him close to me.

I offered him something to drink before he got back on the road. As he stood in the dining room admiring my Annie Lee artwork, I opened a bottle of Heineken for him. As I watched him from the kitchen, I spotted a very distinct birthmark on the side of his right eye, which gave the appearance of three brown teardrops. I took in his ruggedness from his muscular legs up to his AND 1 shorts and sleeveless tee, and biceps that darkened around the outline of his muscles. Trent was a man's man. Even though he was a stranger to me, I knew I wanted him. I wondered, though, if he would still seem like a stranger to me after tonight.

As he reached for the bottle of Heineken, I noticed that his fingertips were a dark brown, almost black, probably from overheated electrical wires. I had an urge to kiss the tip of each one. I wondered what those fingers would feel like inside me. The way he held the bottle and looked me up and down, I wondered if he could tell how bad I wanted him to touch me.

Before I could focus my thoughts, he moved in close to me and, without asking, as if he knew what I needed, he pressed his lips to mine in a soft, slow kiss that felt like butter melting on warm bread. My shoulders went limp, and I was sure he could feel my body give in to him in just that instant. When he tried to pull away and say he was sorry, I pulled him closer. Then, with his lips still slightly touching mine, he asked, "You need this, don't you?" I couldn't answer. Instead, I led him upstairs to my long-empty bedroom, a room I'd closed off since bits of Paulette and Cole had been left there.

Without invitation, he started unbuttoning my cotton shirt. I tried to talk to him, so I could somehow hold on to what little control I had of the situation, but his eyes told me to be quiet. Sitting there on the side of my bed, he started massaging my fingertips and then he took both my hands in his. I lay back on the bed, pulling him with me, and he placed his warm hands on my breasts. His eyes bored deep into mine, challenging me not to look away. But I kept closing my eyes, embarrassed that he was pulling me under his spell. By the time his hands reached my waist, he'd taken his clothes off, and seeing his golden brown body I wanted him to take me. I asked him to do so, but all he said was, "Relax, Sasha."

I still had on my skirt, but instead of removing it he ran his hands up my thighs and slid my panties down. I lay back on the bed, but he wasn't finished yet. Pulling my skirt down over my feet, he began to kiss them. I almost wanted him to stop, the feel of his mouth caressing my soles was too intense; it reminded me too much of Cole. It was probably wrong, but I closed my eyes and imagined Trent was Cole. Maybe that's why I couldn't hide tears that rolled down my face. Trent noticed and covered my body with his, brushing my locs back, telling me he loved me. I was so confused about what I was feeling. I had flashbacks of Paulette standing in my doorway, our eyes locked. I knew I'd never forget the look on her face. Then there was Cole, his black silhouette hovering around my room whispering that he loved me. I wanted to tell Trent to get up from me and run from this room of ghosts, but his hands felt too good—the hands of a stranger trying to erase my past. He caressed me as if I were fragile, something I was so very afraid to be.

Trent began to kiss my breasts while caressing his thighs against mine. He was so good. There were no sounds, except for the whirring of the ceiling fan and his hands moving against my skin. My body was so warm from his touch; maybe his hands really did hold heat. He was taking me to another space.

"Sasha, you're a beautiful woman. You just need to slow down and relax. Take your time. You can't have it all. Baby, you gotta let things go, don't hold on forever."

I was fading away to wherever Trent was taking me and before I knew it I was crying, not hard sobs but weeping.

"What could make a woman like you cry?" Trent whispered against my ear.

"Don't ask me questions, Trent. Just make love to me."

He laid his body on top of mine, straddling me as he began to massage my scalp. Trent was not in a rush. His fingers eased their way in between my locs, and I could feel his fingers on my scalp. He told me not to worry, that he would take care of me. And it soothed me, but at the same time I was more than ready for him to take me.

"Are you sure?" he asked.

"Yes, please."

The next morning I was still surprised to see his long golden body lying in my bed. When the alarm went off, he groggily rolled over, looking for me. He found me in the bathroom doing a quick brush of my teeth and washing my face, hoping to slip back into bed with him.

"What's so funny?" I asked, looking at the broad smile on his face.

"Well, Ms. Sasha, I hope you have a toothbrush for me." I went to pull one out of the medicine cabinet as he strolled naked into the bathroom. He palmed my ass with both hands, and suggested we take a shower together.

While Trent brushed his teeth, I ran the shower and then we climbed in. It seemed like all he wanted to do was savor every inch of my body. And I let him. Let him use his hands to wash me with honey and peppermint shower gel. I could barely stand up, so to break his spell I started squirting him with gel and jumped out. He followed me into the room and it was then that I took him in my mouth and listened to him moan until I could feel his dick pulsating as he exploded inside me.

We lay there exhausted, me sleeping on top of him until my limo arrived and we both had to return to our lives; me to L.A. and Trent to New Jersey.

8

BABYSITTER

I was so happy to see Owen. Little O, who was now two years old, had come to the airport with his dad. He seemed to know who I was because we'd sent many pictures back and forth and tried to spend at least a total of one month together during the year. One of the benefits of working for Phoenix was getting to extend my stay in cities we traveled to for business. This meant I could always see Owen when I was in Los Angeles and Phoenix's company paid my expenses.

Owen looked good. He reminded me so much of his father. Tall, slim, and cocoa brown with strong jawlines. I'd married his father when I was nineteen, and it had lasted a good ten years. That's when he decided he wanted someone with a younger body and more impressionable mind. Thus, he jumped ship and moved to L.A. with his new woman, leaving me behind with Owen. At the age of eight my son became my protector and took over as man of our house. Then about five years ago, when his father had been struck with prostate cancer, Owen moved to L.A.

My son was now a schoolteacher in Compton in the winter and during the summer he managed a community center. Deirdre, his wife, was a nurse's assistant at Cedars Sinai Hospital. Owen's young wife was also from Compton. She was petite, jet black, and had a real ghetto-girl attitude. Deirdre and I hadn't hit it off at first because I thought she was moving a little too fast, getting pregnant and married within a year. But she eventually proved herself, and we'd become close. She even felt comfortable enough about our relationship to call me in Philly one night crying because she'd caught Owen with another woman. Well, that was definitely one of the traits he'd inherited from his father.

Even from a distance Owen had been a strong man for me during the trial. But sometimes he was too tough on me; he had a way of making me face the truth about myself. I'd always known he hadn't approved of my relationship with Cole. I thought that was part of the reason he'd stayed in Los Angeles.

While Owen and Deirdre were at work, I stayed at their crowded two-bedroom apartment with Little O and did day trips. I knew Owen and Deirdre were struggling financially—it wasn't cheap living in L.A., so I helped as much as they would let me. I went grocery shopping and packed their cabinets and freezer. I even replenished their toiletries—and, of course, Little O had to have new clothes. I was just glad that my son didn't complain that I did these things.

*   *   *

To my surprise and delight Trent phoned often during the week and we began getting to know each other. He even surprised me one afternoon by having a florist deliver a beautiful multicolored bouquet of flowers. He was making it so that I couldn't wait to get home.

On my last night in L.A. Owen and I went to dinner at The House of Blues. He asked me how things were going with Phoenix and I told him that I was working hard and that he'd given me a few gifts of appreciation. To my surprise, he told me that when Phoenix last played in Los Angeles he'd taken him and Deirdre to dinner. Phoenix had been good to Owen in the past, too. When Owen had graduated from college last year, Phoenix bought him a Jeep Cherokee. All Owen had to do was pay the insurance, and I took care of that. Phoenix always had a way of making sure all his bases were covered.

When I changed the subject and told Owen about meeting Trent and what a nice guy I thought he was, Owen stopped me in midsentence and asked, "So, how are you really, Mom?"

My eyes immediately began to swell with tears. Owen moved his chair closer to mine.

"Mom, do you still think about what happened?" I couldn't answer because if words came out, so would the tears. He put his arm around me.

"I miss Cole so much. But what I mostly think about is Paulette. I mean, sometimes I can still smell her blood."

"Mom, I'm so sorry I can't be there with you."

I just shook my head. "But I'm getting better. I think

having Trent around will help," I answered, as I thought back to how safe I felt having him in my bed.

"This is the brother you've been talking to every night?"

"Yeah, he's pretty nice."

"Have you told him about what happened?"

Embarrassed, I shook my head no. "Not yet. I wanna wait."

"Well, have you heard from Cole?" he asked. I could tell that he was hoping that I hadn't.

"No, not at all."

All in all it was a good trip—Owen always had a way of making me feel like one day my life would get better and that I'd get rid of the ghosts that haunted me.

On Saturday I flew from LAX to BWI. Trent picked me up from the airport and insisted that I needed help with babysitting Arshell's children. I thought he'd been joking but here he was, and, damn, did he look good. He must've spent the last week in the sun, because his golden color had now turned a deep bronze. I couldn't wait for the opportunity to get next to him.

I thought we'd be going straight to Arshell's, but he had other plans. He drove toward Centennial Park on Route 108. He told me that we were going on a picnic. Now, I liked Trent, but a picnic wasn't what I was looking forward to doing with him. I'd only talked to Phoenix once while in L.A. so my plan was to catch up on work while I was at Arshell's. I tried explaining this to Trent, and he told me to concentrate on my work, that he just wanted to relax and have lunch before we started babysitting.

The park turned out to be a pleasant surprise. Trent

picked a spot near the lake that was filled with ducks and even a few small rowboats. There were children trying to fly kites without wind and adults riding bikes. And it smelled good; dirt, flowers, and the water from the lake stirred the love I'd lost for nature. I couldn't remember the last time I'd been to a park.

Once we were situated I opened my briefcase and pulled out my call sheet. I checked my voice mail and began returning calls and making notes. I watched Trent as I did this, and the more I watched, the more my pace slowed. He had pulled fried chicken wings, a salad, and deviled eggs from a picnic basket. Oh, he was real good. I acted like I wasn't looking as he fixed my plate and doused my wings with hot sauce. Then he pulled an ice cold bottle of Verdi out of his cooler. In the middle of a call with Phoenix's Nike rep, I excused myself, put the phone on mute and asked Trent if he was trying to impress me. He said, "If I was trying to do that, I would've taken you to Short Hills." I wasn't sure what he meant but I was willing to visit his home to find out.

Trent sat close to me while we ate. I told him about my visit with Owen and he was glad I'd had a good time and hoped that he could meet him one day. Then, of course, he had a story about work. He'd been teaching a class and talking about voltage when he suddenly thought of me and said my name. His class fell out in laughter and had been teasing him ever since. He was also excited to tell me that the opportunity for him to run for president of the International Brotherhood of Electrical Workers, IBEW for short, might be closer than he thought.

After we finished eating we lay back on the blanket,

talking about what to do with Arshell's children over the weekend. Trent began nodding off, and I couldn't resist massaging his temples. Before I could get to his shoulders, he sat up and began kissing me. It was hard for both of us to believe this was only our second date.

"I can't believe how much I've missed you," he said, sounding surprised, while nibbling on my earlobe.

"Why not? Aren't I a woman worthy of being missed?" I asked, tracing the birthmark by his eye with my thumb.

"You're more than that, even though I just met you last week."

He looked deep into my eyes and asked, "Sasha, do you know what your name means?"

I raised my eyebrows at his question as if I didn't know the answer.

"Sasha means protector of men."

"Are you saying you need me to protect you?" I was hoping he didn't.

"Only if you're gonna hurt me."

"Now *that* you don't have to worry about." I wondered, though, if he did, because until now I hadn't been able to protect anyone, not even myself.

The weekend with Trent and the children turned out to be the most fun I'd had in a long time. We spent a lot of time at the pool, went to the movies, and Trent even took the twins, Martin and Malcolm, to the D.C. zoo one afternoon while Lisa and I went to Columbia Mall to shop. We returned with presents for everybody.

Our evenings were even better than our days. We'd agreed to sleep in separate rooms, me in Arshell's bed and him in the family room, but we still found ways to be romantic.

One night after the kids were asleep, I sat in the family room with Trent to watch a movie. I'd just washed my hair and Trent had no problem oiling the scalp between each of my locs. His oily hands seemed to replenish all the energy that Phoenix stripped from me. This man was slowly easing me into his love. So there we slept, on the floor of the family room.

The next afternoon the kids cooked lunch for us. Trent lit the grill and they made turkey burgers and french fries. The kids had a planned sleepover that night at their cousins' home in Silver Spring, so Trent and I had the house to ourselves. He insisted that we light the fireplace in Arshell's bedroom, even though it was eighty degrees outside. We turned the central air down to fifty-five and lay in front of the fireplace drinking shots of Stoli and listening to old Teddy Pendergrass CDs. He taught me how and why I should smoke a cigar and to turn him on, I practiced licking a cigar slowly and sucking on its wet tip. We both got so horny and drunk that we fell into deep passionate lovemaking. Somewhere in the middle of it, I found myself telling Trent I loved him. It was not the kind of love you built over years but it was nevertheless a deep affection that I wanted to offer Trent. He whispered in my ear, asking for parts of my body that I'd only shared with Cole. I told him he could have all of me.

Trent gently turned me over, and after kissing up and down my spine, his tongue circled the cheeks of my ass, until I was dripping with longing for him. He slowly entered me where only Cole's dick had gone. I didn't realize how much I'd missed it until that moment. Trent already knew how to talk to me. He'd proved that the first night at my house.

"Sasha, you feel so good. You need everything I have to give to you."

"Please, Trent, give it to me."

"I'm gonna love you, Sasha, but only if you let me." I could only moan in response to his lovemaking.

9

GHOSTS

September 2000

I couldn't bring myself to tell Trent about Cole or what had happened for fear of what he'd think of me, and I certainly couldn't tell him about my secret relationship with Phoenix. Trent made me feel so safe that sometimes I felt if I told him it would somehow redeem and cleanse me. But in reality I knew he would never understand. It had only been two months, so there was no need to rush things.

Arshell couldn't have been happier that I was seeing Trent. She was constantly telling me, with the influence of Wayne R. Wayne, what a good man Trent was and how I deserved to have someone like him. Did they ever stop to think if Trent deserved a woman like me? Arshell emphasized that if I wanted to get serious with Trent, not only would I have to stop sleeping with Phoenix but I'd probably have to quit my job.

I never felt the need to prove myself nor did Trent ever question whether I was a good enough woman for him. I just wanted to enjoy him without all the bullshit of my life back in Philly or what was going on in the NBA. I knew that within a month my life would be going into high gear at the start of basketball season. We managed to spend just enough time together so that we didn't get bored with each other. He'd been to my home again, and we'd done simple things like go to Borders on Germantown Avenue and have dinner at Jake's in Manayunk. The more time I spent with Trent the more I knew that my relationship with Phoenix had to end. I wanted Trent to be a real part of my life.

Trent was always getting on me about not taking him outside of what he called my safety net, so I invited him to a Will Downing concert at the Robin Hood Dell, an amphitheater located in North Philly. Never would I have imagined running into Cole.

During intermission as we were returning through the aisles to our seats, I happened to look up from behind Trent and there he was. All six foot four and color of night that I remembered. For an instant, I forgot about our tragic past and was about to move toward him. But then I noticed the woman seated next to him was actually holding his hand. My instinct was to run to him, but seeing the hesitancy in his eyes, we acknowledged each other with a nod.

After Trent and I reached our seats I realized we had a direct view of Cole and his date. Trent didn't notice my attention to the couple. He just pulled me close to him, asking me if I was cold because my arms had chill bumps. But how could I have been cold when it was so sticky out, so hot that the simplest movement made me sweat. I told him I was fine, but he insisted on draping his jacket around me. I couldn't stop looking at the side of Cole's face, the smooth blackness that was now lightly etched with lines.

Listening to Will Downing sing his rendition of "Hey Girl," I strained to hold back tears, *"wondering if something inside of Cole had died as it had inside of me."* I tried to imagine what his life had been like since that night. There'd never been any closure, and, if given the opportunity, I know *"I would've begged him to stay."*

After the concert my eyes searched the crowd and the parking lot for him, but Cole had vanished.

When Trent and I returned to my house I realized that he had asked me more than once if I was okay. Finally, to get him off my back, I told him I wasn't feeling well. But he kept insisting that something was wrong. I looked at Trent and hated him for trying to love a woman who still loved someone else.

Later that night as we lay in bed watching television, I needed to push Cole from my thoughts; I reached for Trent to make love. And we did, strong and passionate, but it didn't help. I listened as he told me he loved me, but all I could think about was Cole. Afterward, he noticed the faraway look in my eyes that I'd been trying to hide. He sat up and asked, "Where the hell is your head at?"

"I don't know," I whispered, turning my back to him and allowing my thoughts of Cole to consume me. I looked around my room and even though there was carpet and new wallpaper, the room still belonged to Cole and me. I felt that Trent shouldn't even be there. I wanted him to leave and was glad when I heard his heavy breathing, an indication that he was asleep. I knew I wouldn't sleep so I got up and went to the bathroom searching for the Xanax that had helped me sleep just two years ago.

Two days later there was a message on my voice mail from Cole. He wanted to talk. I was scared to return the call, and didn't have to because late that night he called again. Our conversation was very cautious. We asked each other the same questions repeatedly, and it was obvious we wanted to meet. I couldn't bear for him to come back into my home so he invited me to his friend's apartment in Bear, Delaware. We made plans to meet there the following evening.

I considered calling Arshell and asking her advice but I knew she'd advise me against seeing Cole. I told myself that I could handle it. I figured I'd wait and tell her about my meeting with Cole afterward. Oddly, I wasn't sure why I was meeting him. Did I expect a reconciliation, or was this meeting going to finally bring closure to our past? Whatever the answer, I wouldn't know until I talked to Cole.

The next day he called and gave me directions to his friend's house. No more, no less. Earlier that day I had a manicure and pedicure, and went to the hairdresser to have my locs set on rods so they could be curly, the way Cole used to like it. I purchased three new outfits, eventually deciding to wear a faded denim skirt and sleeveless sweater. If nothing else, I wanted Cole to remember us like we were.

I arrived at his friend's house at 7:30 in the evening

and was too nervous to get out of the truck. The entire trip I kept second-guessing my decision to see him. Why was I seeing Cole when Trent was in my life—there was no need for me to go backward. I mean, I'd just started sleeping in my bedroom again. But as soon as I saw Cole standing on the balcony smiling at me I relaxed and went to him.

The apartment was clearly a hideout spot for someone. As I walked inside I took note of its sparse furnishings, but I was soon distracted by the delicious aromas coming from the kitchen. I was surprised to see that Cole had cooked. He'd fried flounder, baked macaroni, and steamed broccoli, a familiar meal for the two of us. But this was not the Cole I knew. In the five years we'd been together he'd never done anything in my kitchen except eat. I guess he'd become self-sufficient since his wife died. While he set the table we made small talk about the weather. When I went to sit down, he stepped between the chair and me. Without thinking I stepped into him— all of him. All three years—all of it just flooded back to me. We stood there with me touching his bald head, kissing all over his face, not believing I was this close to him again. Then he pulled away from me, told me to slow down, that he wanted to talk. What was there to talk about? I didn't want to talk about how it had been over the last few years, didn't want to hear how hard it had been on him to lose his son. All of that would hurt too much.

Sitting across from Cole and watching him eat was torture. Every nerve in my body wanted him, but I didn't want to be rejected. And so we began to talk. I found out that he'd been keeping track of me and he wanted to know more about my job with Phoenix. That seemed safe to talk about, so I rambled on until he interrupted and asked, "I hope you aren't fucking that boy, Sasha."

I lowered my head slightly. "Cole, why would you ask me that?"

"'Cause I know what you're capable of."

"Well, I'm not," I lied. I knew he didn't believe me.

After dinner Cole began to talk about his son. As I helped him clean up the dishes, he told me that his son had been living with his grandmother for two years. He'd recently turned seventeen and had decided to move back in with Cole until he went off to college. They were now reestablishing their relationship. He claimed that Cole Jr. wanted to know about me and the reason why I'd been in his life. I learned that Cole had sold his house in North Philly, moved to the Northeast and was surprised that I hadn't moved out of mine. I admitted that I'd never moved or changed my phone number because I'd always wanted him to be able to reach me.

Cole was silent for a moment, so I asked the question that had been bothering me.

"Cole, why am I here?" I asked. I couldn't help sounding impatient.

"Why'd you come?" Cole demanded harshly. "Are you surprised that I haven't tried to fuck you yet?"

I turned away from him, shocked by his mean tone. Trying to answer him, I whispered, "No, it's not that. It's just—"

"Just what? You think we can just forget about what happened?" he asked, moving toward me. There was something about the way his body had tightened that was scaring me. I slowly stepped back but he grabbed me, almost violently, by the arm. I tried to pull away from him but he squeezed tighter.

"Maybe I should go," I said. I leaned back against the stove.

"Why, Sasha? I'm about to give you what you came for."

This wasn't the Cole I'd known or was expecting. He'd never been violent. But maybe since the suicide of his wife, anything was possible.

"Cole, what the fuck is wrong with you?" I countered, trying not to let my fear show.

Grabbing a handful of my hair, he pulled me to him, opening his mouth to cover my lips with his. He started talking, almost in a whisper.

"Sasha, I need you. You don't know what it's like for me." I could feel the tenseness in his body as he held me.

I pleaded, "Cole, please, not like this."

"You know how many times I've wanted to call you? How many times I drove past your house?"

His arms around me were so tight I could hardly breathe. I tried to wriggle myself free, but he began pulling at the snap on my denim skirt. It popped open, and he unzipped my skirt and pushed it to the floor. Before I could reach for it, Cole dropped to his knees, grabbing and holding on to my hips. Through my panties he pressed my pulsating pussy against his face. I closed my eyes and felt my body weaken. His need drained me. He said my name over and over, mixing it with the sound his mouth was making against the warm juices that ran from me.

He picked me up, carried me into the bedroom and spread me onto the bed. He didn't move, didn't say anything, just stared at me. I reached up from the bed, pulled him by the waist, and unzipped his pants. He never took the time to take his boxers off, just pulled his dick out of the opening and pushed himself far up inside me. I screamed his name as he pounded my body with his hardness. It was scary, this ravenous passion. I found myself begging for him to stop; it was too much for me. But all he did was call my name and tell me he loved me over and over. Finally, just when I thought he was slowing down, he let himself come into me.

There was no sleeping. He wanted to take me over and over, and I wanted him to have me. We must have finally slept, because I awoke to the sound of running water. I called his name and followed the sound of his voice into the bathroom, where he sat in the bathtub filled with a sweet musk scent. I climbed in and he took my toes, one at a time, and kissed them. Cole seemed to have missed every inch of me, as I'd missed him.

As I lay in bed on Saturday morning watching Cole sleeping, I was determined for us to be together. I decided to fix breakfast, so I dressed and drove to the store for a few items. I had arrived at Cole's the night before and since being there I hadn't answered my cell phone or checked my messages. I didn't want anything to interrupt the time we had together. At the moment, nothing existed outside of Cole's make-believe home. While I was gone I phoned Trent and Phoenix and retrieved my messages. Phoenix, of course, was bitching about not being able to reach me all night. I interrupted his little tirade and reminded him that I did have a personal life. Trent, on the other hand, was cool. He just thought I'd probably been tied up working with Phoenix.

The other call I made was to Arshell, who was actually more understanding of my meeting with Cole than I expected. The only thing she didn't agree with me about was that Cole and I actually had a chance at a future together. I dismissed her negativity and told her that I had to go. As far as I was concerned, now that Paulette was gone and three years had passed, nothing could stop us.

When I returned to the apartment, I could hear Cole on the phone with his son. I began cooking a breakfast of turkey sage sausage, home fries, and eggs scrambled lightly with cheese, just how he liked it. We even had orange juice and fresh coffee. As I stood in the kitchen turning the potatoes, I could feel Cole watching me. He walked toward me smiling and wrapped his arms around my waist, holding my hands as I flipped the sausage. When he nuzzled his face in the crevice of my neck, I felt I could've stayed in Delaware forever. We didn't talk, just stood there cooking together in an embrace that I had never forgotten.

After breakfast we talked nonstop about our changed lives. Because of all the publicity, Cole had changed jobs. Instead of teaching at a high school he was now counseling abused children. He said it was very hard to find someone special because he always found himself searching for a woman made up of Paulette and me. How sad. I, of course, couldn't tell him about my affair with Phoenix but I did tell him about Trent.

Sunday arrived too soon. We had yet to talk about our future together. Cole kept changing the subject every time I brought it up. I was beginning to think that he no longer loved me. After brunch, watching a movie, and making love in the daylight on the balcony, we lay on the couch, wrapped in each other, carefully broaching the subject of our being back together.

"I know this isn't gonna be easy for us to talk about," Cole said.

"It depends on what you want the outcome to be."

"Sasha, you have to understand the consequences of what our being back together would mean."

I turned to face him. "It means that we love each other. Right?"

His sadness was evident in his voice. "Sasha, baby, you don't understand."

I didn't understand and I wasn't willing to give up that easy.

"Look, we could . . . maybe we could just start out slow. Isn't that what we always wanted, not to have to hide? Cole, I know we can make it work. We could even move away once your son leaves for college." I was begging him.

"Sasha, Sasha, it's not that easy, baby."

"What's not easy? What is it, Cole? Are you scared?"

"Look, I love you, girl. You know that. But I am afraid. I'm afraid of who might get hurt. Our love is too strong, baby. We love so hard that we forget about everybody around us."

"But there's nobody there anymore. Cole, you just have to want it more than you're afraid of it." I didn't want to hear what he was telling me and tried to break his embrace but he held on.

"Who cares about anybody around us?" I asked, even though I knew what his answer would be.

He held my face so I was forced to look at him. "Yeah, but what about my son?"

My eyes swelled with tears while Cole gently talked to me.

"Don't cry, Sasha. Please don't cry 'cause we can't be together. Just be happy that we know what it's really like to love someone. Sometimes . . . two people can't always share that love with each other. Please tell me you understand."

At some level his words began to penetrate. I couldn't fight Cole's reasoning anymore. He'd worn me down and I was so tired that my thoughts were late in responding to him, so I gave up.

10

HAPPY HOLIDAYS

October 2000

After spending the weekend with Cole I couldn't wait to see Trent. It would be the first time I'd gone to his condo in Short Hills. As I drove up the New Jersey Turnpike my mind twisted and turned, trying to figure out how I could still love Cole.

Trent's two-story condo was located in a gated community surrounded by trees and a man-made lake. His apartment had a large deck with a view of the surrounding pines, and, inside, his furnishings made it apparent that he'd spent a lot of time shopping at Restoration Hardware. He was definitely into art, and surprisingly some of it was his own. He had an entire room dedicated to his book collection. I was pleased to discover that Trent could cook. He fixed us a meal of porterhouse steak, stewed tomatoes, and rice. I was impressed.

To see how much we really did like each other, we decided to play house for a week. I packed up my laptop and any paperwork I'd need to keep on top of my work with Phoenix and made myself comfortable in his condo. Trent was very easy to be with. He wasn't demanding or too needy. I realized I had no choice. I had to be with him because he was the only man who would admit to loving me publicly. And who knows, maybe if this worked out I could one day become Mrs. Trent Russell.

I stayed inside much of the week except for a trip to the mall. During the day I worked the phone setting up Phoenix's final travel schedule before the season started. I enjoyed my time with Trent. He brought me breakfast in bed, and I took great pleasure in packing his lunch every morning.

It was a turn-on for me to watch him get dressed in his white hard hat and faded jeans that were just tight enough to see his ass and hug his thighs. Each morning he'd tuck his lunch cooler under his arm, kiss me, and walk out the door with a swagger that twice made me beg him to turn around and take me again before he went to work. He'd just laugh and call me crazy.

In the evenings I cooked big dinners—like stuffed chicken breasts, greens, mashed potatoes—and I always wore something sexy, usually just one of his button-down dress shirts. One night I surprised him by turning the dining room into a strip club and dancing for him on the table while he stuck dollar bills into my garter. We wound up not eating dinner until midnight.

I didn't know if it was better watching him get ready

to go to work or waiting for him to come home. I enjoyed the smell of him when he came home from work. I liked him sweaty and musky, and I'd take him before he showered 'cause sometimes I couldn't wait and wanted that smell all over me. I could learn to love Trent. He wasn't smooth like Cole, or a roughrider like Phoenix, but he was all that a woman could want.

The only thing I didn't like were the hours in between his comings and goings. I spent that time alone, often thinking about how Cole had gotten into my pores in just one weekend. He had taken over my thoughts and I couldn't seem to stop wanting him. I had to force myself not to page him or call his home number, which he'd given to me in case of an emergency. The only emergency I could imagine would be . . . that I wanted him, needed him.

It wasn't easy at the end of the week, moving from Cole to Trent to Phoenix, but I had to because it was what had become of my life. Maybe having so much sex was my way of trying to fill some empty emotions. My life was no longer my own. All I did was satisfy the men who desired me.

My trip with Phoenix to the Midwest marked the first time I literally slept with him and did what he wanted every night, every day, no matter how many times. I'd never been with him so freely before because I always needed that space to remind me that this really wasn't a relationship. Some nights I was uneasy having him beside me and I'd roll over to the edge of the bed. I began to realize that the idea of sex equaling love was not adding up.

During this trip I told Phoenix about Trent. He

seemed genuinely happy for me, but I sensed he could not have cared less as long as he got what he wanted. It was a trade-off—I gave Phoenix everything he wanted and in return he shopped for me, in every city, Dallas, Indianapolis, Portland. I didn't even think about what I was buying; I just spent his money. And it wasn't just clothes. I bought things for my house and had them shipped, and as my private cash bonuses increased, out of guilt probably more than love, I bought Trent a diamond-faced Cartier watch.

The only person I didn't keep secrets from was Arshell. She knew the madness my life had become and often I'd just be quiet and listen to her tell me, without arguing, that I couldn't go on fucking both Trent and Phoenix forever, that not dealing with the situation was like spitting in the wind.

Arshell had met Phoenix a few times but we never really had a chance to sit and talk, just the three of us. Phoenix was well aware that Arshell knew all my secrets, especially what I was doing with him. Arshell was the only person Phoenix and I could be comfortable with to talk about our affair. After one of his preseason games at the MCI center in D.C., the three of us went to dinner at Georgia Brown's.

Arshell and Phoenix talked about sports at length since she was a sports buff. Basketball, football, and baseball, she was more knowledgeable than I, and I worked in the industry. Phoenix often teased her about being a coach-in-training. While they talked I ordered appetizers and drinks.

Arshell teased him that he was "turning me out" and that pretty soon she might want to get her own young boy. Phoenix told her that he was the one turned out. Then, for once, Phoenix got serious and told Arshell that being with me was about more than sex. He felt that I was the only woman outside of Crystal who didn't want him for his money, that I actually wanted to see him make something of himself.

"Arshell, you don't know what Sasha does for me. She takes care of my shit and gives me good head."

"I hate you, Phoenix Carter," I chimed in.

"Damn," Arshell said.

"No, I'm serious. She know I love her." He was always saying that and I tried not to hear it.

Laughing, Arshell added, "Well, then. Maybe I should be getting paid for keeping such a big secret out of the *National Enquirer.* 'NBA athlete Phoenix Carter is sleeping with his personal assistant, Sasha Borianni.'"

"Yo, what you want, Ar?" Phoenix asked, probably ready to buy her, too.

"I don't want anything. Just make sure you take care of my girl," she shot back.

Turning to look at me, Phoenix said, "Don't worry. She's always gonna be taken care of. Sasha knows she's down for life. I swear on my children."

That night my thoughts turned to Trent. He certainly wasn't the perfect man, even though at times it seemed so, I guess because I was so imperfect. Since we never had the conversation of whether or not either of us was seeing anyone else, it was only a matter of time before I found out about Paige. After my trip with Phoenix, instead of returning to Philly, Trent convinced me to come to New Jersey.

I was alone at Trent's condo one afternoon after he'd

been called out during a storm because of downed electrical wires. While I sat in bed flipping through an *InStyle*
magazine, the phone rang. I usually didn't answer his
phone, but when the answering machine clicked on and I
heard a woman's voice cursing him out and asking for me,
I picked up the receiver. The woman was stunned at first
to hear my voice, then she asked my name.

"Ms. Borianni," I stated.

"Well I'm Paige and you're the one Trent's been seeing," she said, all in one breath.

"Are you asking me or telling me?" I asked, fucking
with her.

"Look, I think we need to talk."

Feeling confident that I was Trent's woman, I
answered, "I can't imagine what we have to talk about."

"For starters, I'm carrying Trent's baby."

On that note I agreed to talk with her. To my surprise
she lived in Trent's complex, so it was only a matter of
minutes before she arrived. Well, Paige was clearly pregnant, almost six months, and to top it off she was all
that. You know the type, about five-eight, light-skinned,
hair bouncing and behaving, and probably a size eight
shoe.

Paige wasn't a young girl, either. I suspected she was
thirty-five. She told me she worked as a consultant for an
architectural firm; that's how she'd met Trent. She
strolled into Trent's condo wearing a long-sleeve, navy
blue, Donna Karan knit dress that made her the sexiest
pregnant woman I'd ever seen. I noticed she moved
around his place with ease, as if she were very familiar
with it.

"I see you've made yourself comfortable here," she said

looking around at my things, which were spread throughout Trent's place.

"There was nothing to stop me."

"Listen, Sasha, I didn't come here to fight with you. I just thought you should know that you're not the only woman in Trent's life."

"Honey, we're never the only woman in any man's life. Now, you came here for a reason?"

She sat down on the couch and I remained standing.

"Trent will probably never admit to this, but we've been dating for two years. We even got engaged," she said, flashing me her diamond ring.

"Typical reaction I guess, from a responsible man when he's told he's about to become a father," I said, trying to hide my surprise with what she was telling me.

"Typical, maybe, until you came along. That's when he started questioning whether he was really the father of our child."

"I'm assuming he told you about us and now you're blaming me."

"No, not really. Trent is his own man."

"What's the status of your relationship with him?"

"He wants a paternity test once the baby comes, but what you really should know is that we're still sleeping together."

"I see."

"As recent as last week if you should know."

"Is that it?" I asked and then started walking toward the door.

"Not unless you have some questions."

"Anything else I need to know I can find out from Trent. Good night."

Closing the door behind Paige I thought about the new twist my life was taking. While I was having an affair with Phoenix, I'd had no idea Trent was this involved with anyone else. The difference between us, though, was I hadn't allowed myself to get caught. Somehow, knowing he had Paige made me feel less guilty about what I was doing. How could I argue that he was doing wrong by me? Neither of us had been honest. Just because we said we loved each other didn't mean we were committed. What was this commitment thing about anyway? People were always saying that a woman couldn't do the same things as a man and still be a woman. But why not? Why couldn't a woman have sex with multiple men and just do it because she enjoyed it? There didn't always have to be a story of incest, rape, and abuse. At times I certainly thought I enjoyed it. There was something about the way I could flip-flop between men that simply turned me on.

About one in the morning Trent returned home. I was in bed, so I waited until he climbed in beside me before I sat up and confronted him.

"So, you want to tell me about your baby momma?"

"Uh, what are you talking about, Sasha? Come on, lay down, woman, so we can get some sleep."

"Paige came over today. Are you gonna tell me what's up or not?"

His body stiffened but he wouldn't turn around to face me.

"What'd she tell you?"

"Damn what she told me. I wanna hear what you have to say."

He sat up, his back against the headboard. He didn't say anything for a few minutes and then he went into the same story she'd told me, with the addition that she was sleeping with someone else. That's why he'd questioned the baby being his. Somehow I didn't believe him.

"And that's it? You're not still fucking her, like last week?"

"Sasha, are you crazy? I wouldn't do no shit like that. What kind of man do you think I am? I told you it's probably not even my baby."

"I don't give a damn who the father of the baby is. I just want to know why you haven't told me you've been fucking another bitch, especially since we've stopped using condoms."

I know he was surprised at my outburst, but it happened faster than I could control it.

"I swear to you, Sasha, I don't want that woman. Now please cut all this shit out and go to sleep."

I watched him while he fidgeted, trying to sleep and probably wondering if I was done. He was so predictable that I almost laughed at him. I knew then that despite all of Trent's good qualities, he was still a dog-ass nigga, like all the other men I knew. Which made me like him even more.

Now that I knew there was another woman in the picture, I was determined to make Trent mine. He'd been asking me to spend Christmas with his family in New York, but I'd kept putting him off by saying that I wasn't ready to meet his family yet. But after meeting Paige I changed my mind. I agreed to meet his family and I suggested he meet mine, too. At the end of the week we drove to Philly where we had dinner with my daddy. Trent got a kick out of listening to Daddy brag about how at the age of sixteen I'd been a woman and taken care of him. He and

Trent had no problem getting along. They sat around talking about my father's women and smoking cigars. I knew my father liked him because he kept asking me if he was finally gonna have another son-in-law.

That weekend Trent and I flew to L.A. so he could meet Owen, and the four of us had dinner at Spago. Owen was impressed and pulled me to the side to tell me that Trent was a good man and that I'd better not lose him. On the other hand, when talking to Owen alone I found him questioning my relationship with Phoenix. I sensed that he knew our relationship was more than business because of all the extra things I'd been doing for him and his family, but there was no way I could admit it. I was just glad to have the approval of the two most important men in my life. They affirmed that Trent was the man for me.

During our trip to L.A., I began to realize that I really did love Trent and he expressed those same feelings. The biggest question was what to do with them. We'd gone sailing one afternoon and there on the deck we talked about Paige and his responsibility. He practically admitted that the baby was his but because of our relationship he wanted to be certain. I reassured him that I would still be there for him. Once we were back on shore Trent went out shopping for some imported cigars and I called Arshell to talk about how I was feeling. I was confused by my love for Trent and I was scared to share my secrets with him. The two of us decided it was best to ease Phoenix out of my life. Arshell insisted that there was no easy way to end my sexual relationship with Phoenix, that I'd just have to quit. As for my past with Cole, she was confident that Trent would understand.

I tested the waters and shared with Trent that I was tiring of my job with Phoenix. Trent admitted that he didn't like how Phoenix demanded so much of my time and felt that I could service him just as well from my home in Philly and not be so dominated by him.

We arrived back in New Jersey two days before Christmas, and from there I flew to D.C. for a meeting with a potential new endorser. Then it was on to New York for Christmas dinner with Trent's family. I don't know why I was so nervous. Maybe because I was also meeting his daughter. I wondered if his family would question where my and Trent's future was headed. It wasn't that I didn't want a future with Trent, but I was scared to let go of my past.

Trent wanted to get to New York early but a surprise call from Paige held us up. She was now ready to make demands. It seemed Paige was asking for money. But from the tone of his conversation I could tell she wanted more than money; she wanted him.

Since Trent's truck was in the shop we drove my Lexus. By now, the original had been replaced with a black-on-black 2001 model, which I hoped didn't appear grandiose to Trent's family. I was careful not to overdress and just wore a simple Calvin Klein pantsuit. I had my locs pulled up in a ponytail; I wore silver hoop earrings and a silver Coach watch I'd gotten from Trent. I consciously wore nothing that I'd received as a gift from Phoenix. I wanted it to be clear that I was Trent's woman.

Trent's parents were really nice even though we didn't have much time to sit and talk, as they were busy preparing dinner. I envied how Trent interacted with his family and how everyone simply enjoyed being together. After dinner, I found myself sitting between his two sisters while everyone was eating dessert. One of them was an underwriter for an insurance company and the other a legal secretary. They didn't ask me about my relationship with Trent but were more interested in Phoenix. They wanted to know exactly what I did for him and what he was like off the court.

As with all women who envied my position, Trent's sisters wanted to know how I could resist a millionaire who was fine, young, and probably a stallion in bed. Phoenix had recently appeared on the cover of *Code* magazine so the image of his body was fresh in their minds. They couldn't imagine my not being attracted to him, regardless of the age difference. So instead of telling them I was totally uninterested in Phoenix, I told them that at first I was excited, but quickly forgot about his good looks because he was such a slave driver. They also asked the standard question of why young boys spent so much money on cars and jewelry. It was so funny how people always wanted to know the intimate details of a celebrity's life. They even tried to find out how much money I made, but I steered them away from that subject by telling them it wasn't enough for the services I performed.

When it came time to open gifts, I knew Trent had gone overboard when I saw the blue Tiffany box. I just prayed it wasn't a ring. Instead, he'd bought me a diamond anklet. I knew it was expensive by the size of the diamonds and by the reaction from his sisters. I just hoped Trent wasn't trying to compete with Phoenix. My gift to Trent was more practical: I gave him two boxes, one with a humidor he'd been admiring and the other held a pair of Prada boots.

Trent's daughter, Briana, had kept to herself during most of my visit. I moved away from Trent's sisters when I looked up and saw Briana enter the room. She was tall like her dad but probably looked more like her mother. What she did have of her father's was his birthmark, and it added to her young beauty. I could tell Trent was proud of her and I was glad that, at Arshell's suggestion, I'd also brought her a gift, a $100 Gap gift certificate.

Trent made sure Briana and I spent some time alone to get to know each other. We talked about school and boys, but she, too, was more interested in Phoenix. She had her girlfriend with her, and she wanted to know if she could ever meet Phoenix. I surprised them both and called Phoenix on his cell phone so Briana could talk to him. Realizing she was Trent's daughter, Phoenix invited her and her girlfriend to spend the weekend at his house in Florida. Briana was ecstatic.

11

COCONUT GROVE

March 2001

Now that we'd made it through the holidays and the wild All-Star weekend in Detroit, basketball season was in full swing. Phoenix, though, was on the injured list with a slightly sprained ankle. Chicago was playing New Jersey, and I was in New York with him for two days for a series of meetings at the NBA league office. Phoenix was well aware of my relationship with Trent and had wanted to meet him but I kept putting him off, warning him that Trent and I were getting serious and I needed to let our thing go. But he refused. So when I accepted his offer to drive me to Trent's, I could tell he was curious to meet the man who was taking my attention away from him.

Once we reached Trent's complex and parked, I rang

the bell. Trent opened the door with a wide smile and gave me juicy kiss, I'm sure for Phoenix's sake. Out of the corner of my eye I could tell that Phoenix was checking Trent out. I was happy to show Trent off—his shoulders almost filled the doorway, and he had a smile and open arms for me. I kissed Trent, first on the lips and then on his birthmark, which had become my habit. I introduced them, and they shook hands in the normal Black man greeting and Trent invited us in. I thought Phoenix would decline but he stepped through the doorway.

I went upstairs to put my bags away, leaving them downstairs. As I moved about upstairs I kept my ears open to their conversation. I could hear Phoenix questioning Trent about dumb shit—his CD collection, his job, even me. I knew Trent noticed Phoenix's fishing for information; I just hoped he didn't know why. My hope that Phoenix would soon be leaving was dashed when he accepted Trent's invitation to stay for dinner.

When Trent went into the kitchen, I asked Phoenix what he thought he was doing.

"I just wanna get to know the nigga and make sure you alright."

"Shit, I'm forty years old and can take care of myself. What do you know? You ain't but twenty-five."

Phoenix slid down into a dining-room chair and grabbed his dick, as was his habit when he was trying to make a point. "I know one thing, and that's what we did at my house last night means you're not that fucking serious about Mr. Trent."

I would never admit it but he was right. Just the night before he'd had me in such a state of ecstasy that I'd begged him to fuck me.

"I hate you, Phoenix Carter." He gave me a sly grin as Trent reentered the room.

So there we sat at the table, the three of us having dinner. After a while it wasn't so bad. Phoenix made a point of confirming our visit with Briana at his home in Florida. After dinner the two of them mostly talked about sports. Phoenix was surprised that Trent hadn't been to one of his games yet. And Trent asked Phoenix how he handled all the pressure of his female groupies. I listened as Phoenix boasted about his lifestyle, as if he were really confident with who he was. I knew better. I had seen a side of Phoenix that he hid from everyone, even Crystal. Phoenix suffered from a bad case of insecurity. He often admitted to me, sometimes in tears, that he couldn't take the pressure of being a superstar, of having his private life invaded by the world. He didn't like people scrutinizing every play he made on the court and every move he made off the court.

Phoenix happily rambled on about all the sluts he'd been with. Then in a smart-ass move, he said to Trent, "Ask Sasha, she knows how women be all over me." And I did know, but I just shook my head in disgust.

Contrary to his often-brash attitude and our twisted relationship, I did have a genuine love of basketball and actually enjoyed watching Phoenix play. His ego was big enough so I never told him how much his on-court performance turned me on. There was just something about the way he went to the foul line. His shoulders tightened, and he would rock back on his heels, then forward on his toes, then his muscular arms contracted as he sent the ball floating to the net.

Looking around the table at our threesome, I realized

I had always been good at betraying people. I knew it wasn't right. Trent didn't deserve to be part of my web of affairs. The strange thing about my relationship with these two men was that sometimes after I'd been with Phoenix, I wanted Trent even more. Why had I turned out like this? I'd never planned on being a bad girl. The good girls had always taken my boyfriends when I was young. They were always prettier and smarter and had a mother. But me, I had been raised by a hustling limo driver whose values weren't—and couldn't be—the same as those in a two-parent household. But whose fault was it really? My father had done his best so there really was no blaming him. It was I who'd made all the wrong choices.

The following weekend, the four of us—Trent, Briana, her girlfriend, and I—arrived at Sarasota International. To make the trip special, I'd reserved a limo to pick us up at the airport. I wanted to do my best not only to impress Briana but to give her a lot to tell her friends back home. Phoenix was due in Chicago on Sunday afternoon, so we had to make the best of our short visit.

As we pulled up to Phoenix's Coconut Grove estate, I was more concerned about what Trent might be thinking. He was aware I worked among money, but I wasn't sure if he could deal with it up close and personal. Crystal set us up in the guesthouse, which had four bedrooms and was more like a mini mansion. The kids had a great time swimming with Trent and Phoenix while Crystal and I barbequed. Phoenix offered to fly us to Disney World on Saturday morning, but the girls preferred to stay at the house. As with his home in Chicago, Phoenix had a fully furnished game room—a pool table, video games, Ping-

Pong, and a theater-sized television that offered all the current movies.

On Saturday night, Crystal's nanny came over so the four of us could go out. We chartered a plane, flew to South Beach, and had dinner at a private club. There we met up with Phoenix's celebrity counterparts. Phoenix impressed Trent by introducing him as his "ole head," rather than as my man. When Phoenix and I found ourselves alone I thanked him for inviting us down. I was glad that he and Trent were getting along. He just laughed and told me, "We should. Shit, we got enough in common."

"The only thing you have in common is me."

"That's about enough, ain't it, Sasha?" he asked while pouring from one of the bottles of Moët he'd ordered.

"One day, Phoenix, I'm not gonna be fucking your arrogant ass anymore."

"Oh yeah? When's that gonna be?"

Later that night when Trent and I had finished making love, he told me there were a few things we needed to talk about. First he felt it was finally time for him to begin his run for IBEW president for the local union in Paramus, New Jersey. His campaign would involve fund-raising, meetings with some Italian Mafia types, and a lot of political bullshit. I was happy for him because I knew this was what he'd wanted. I was happy, that is, until he gave me the second half of his news. Paige had delivered a baby boy and Trent had been there. I was furious that he'd kept it from me, and the worst part was that he was the father and planned to take an active role. Pissed off that he'd kept it a secret, I chose to sleep downstairs on the couch and almost wished I could've gone to Phoenix.

As I lay there on the couch I realized how truly fucked up my life was. Maybe I really wasn't anybody's woman. Here Trent had a daughter, and now a son, that would take up parts of his life where I couldn't even compete. And what did I really have with Phoenix? Maybe I needed to remove myself from both relationships. Maybe I just wasn't good enough to belong to any one man.

There never seemed to be one man solely for me anyway. How long would I continue to envy other women for what seemed to come so easily to them and so hard to me? Why was I always left feeling like a penny waiting for change? I even resented my mother for leaving me. How could she go, how could God take her knowing I'd be so alone? Left alone to understand why men wanted me, and why I always attached myself to the ones who belonged to someone else. My daddy had cheated on her; I'd read it in her diary. She'd painfully accepted it as if it were part of marriage because he was good to her. She was the reason I'd moved to Chestnut Hill in the first place, 'cause she'd written about it, that it was, "a quiet old town that seemed to let you live a slower life compared to West Philly." If only she'd written more for me. Maybe I could've learned some lessons a girl can only get from a mother. As hard as I tried, I could never imagine her voice or her touch. I knew she was pretty; we even looked alike. But no matter how much of her diary I read, or the number of pictures I stared into, I still couldn't find the woman who was supposed to be my mother.

With the news of Trent's baby, I changed my return flight from New Jersey and flew into Philly. Arriving at home Monday morning I found a note from Robertson's florist who had attempted to make a delivery. I drove over to the florist's shop on Germantown Avenue, thinking that Trent was trying to make up with me. But instead of the dozen multicolored roses Trent usually sent, I found an arrangement of exotic flowers. And instead of the card being signed "Love, Trent," it read, "Because I'll never stop loving you." It was signed "A Dark Stranger." I knew that it could only be from Cole.

I decided to let Trent spend some time with his new son. Phoenix's schedule was fully focused on basketball because of the playoffs, so I worked from home.

I stayed in Philly for three weeks, doing all the things I hadn't done in a long time. I visited Daddy, shopped in Center City, read three books, cooked comfort foods, and reacquainted myself with my home. I even took out time to go downtown to Total Serenity for a full day of spa treatment. By the end of the three weeks, Trent was begging me to come to New Jersey, and I found myself yearning to see him.

I drove to Short Hills on a stormy Thursday afternoon and decided during the ride that I would begin to accept Trent's son as part of my life. Now, I needed to find a way to end it with Phoenix. Trent must've seen me parking my truck because he was at the door when I walked up. When I entered the condo I could smell the pasta he was cooking. Before I could head for the kitchen, he stepped into my path, pulled my hands behind me, and handcuffed me.

"C'mon, Trent. Stop playing, I'm tired." I was exhausted from my drive through the turnpike traffic and irritated about all the decisions I'd needed to make.

"You should be. You been gone for three damn weeks." he said.

Encumbered by the cuffs, I slowly followed him into the kitchen. "Trent, please take these off. I have to pee."

Instead of removing them, he led me into the bathroom. He lifted up my skirt, pulled down my tights and panties and asked me if I needed help sitting down. I sat and peed while he watched. He never cracked a smile. When I was finished he pulled toilet paper from the holder, wiped my ass front to back, adjusted my clothes, and washed his hands.

Now I was pissed. Stumbling into the kitchen, the smell of pasta sauce mixed with garlic and pesto made my stomach growl. I stood next to him as he stirred and tasted the food.

"Trent, can you take this shit off?"

He ignored me. I bitched, frustrated that I couldn't put my hands on my hips.

"Damn, nigga. If you didn't want me here then maybe I should've stayed the fuck in Philly."

"Who the fuck you talking to like that, Sasha?" he asked. "What do you think, I'm one of them fucking thugs you run around with?" Before I could say another word, he spun me around and grabbed me by the handcuffs.

"You think you're the one running this relationship? That you can just pull away from me without talking about how I feel? Huh, Sasha, is that what you think?" Despite his harsh words, Trent was gentle with me. Holding my arms up he backed me against the table, practically bending me in half. He leaned into me and yanked up my long wool skirt.

"Trent, what the fuck is wrong with you?" I asked with feigned outrage, all the while wondering how this kinky side of him had gone undetected.

Instead of answering, I could hear him pull up a chair behind me. He moved down my body, then I felt him tasting me, right through my panties and tights. He was sucking so hard that I could hear my tights tearing. I wanted to turn around, grab his head, and push his face closer, but his arms were around my waist, pinning me to the table, keeping me from moving.

Suddenly he pushed away from me and cried, "Sasha, you're fucked up. How could you stay away from me? You know I love you. Paige don't mean shit to me. You hear me?"

"Yes, Trent, I'm sorry." I heard him open a kitchen drawer. I had no idea what he was doing until I felt him cutting away at my tights and panties. "Oh God," I moaned.

"You better call somebody 'cause I'm getting ready to fuck the shit outta you."

By now he was on his knees. He inserted two fingers inside me and teased my swollen clit with his tongue. "Please, please, Trent!" I begged. I wanted all of him inside me and urged him to remove the cuffs. He refused until, finally, the juices that flowed from me were running down my thighs. Roughly, he spread my legs apart with his knees and shoved his golden hardness so deep inside me that my knees buckled. But he held me up and spread me out over the kitchen table until he collapsed on top of me.

12

HAPPY BIRTHDAY

May 2001

The more I tried to separate myself from the sordid business and personal relationship Phoenix and I were in, the more I was sucked in deeper. I never romanticized about what could be. It wasn't like we loved each other and wanted a life together. It was just that I couldn't pull myself away from him.

Phoenix had recently played a playoff game in Philly with a layover for two nights, both of which he decided to spend at my house instead of at the Four Seasons with his team. He didn't want to go out, just lie around and have me wait on him, as if I didn't do enough of that as his assistant. It was times like these, when we were intimate, that I could get him to agree to business ideas that he'd otherwise reject. I was constantly telling him that he had to be open-minded about the opportunities that didn't bring him money but offered exposure. Carter Enterprises had expanded and would soon be offering a clothing line. I'd made him subscribe to the *Wall Street Journal, Fortune,* and *Black Enterprise.* He even took my suggestion to get a personal chef, college tutor, and media trainer. He would now be able to take advantage of his sound bites and make the most of his television appearances. Phoenix knew how to dress, but I hired a stylist and tailor to help him refine his look by making sure he had crisp white monogrammed shirts and the latest designs. Even though he had expensive shoes, I forced Phoenix to make sure they were always shined, even if he had to do it himself. Phoenix was slowly transforming from a thug, all about money, to a young entrepreneur learning how to make smart investments. His innate business acumen allowed him to manipulate business meetings dressed like a thug but with the mannerisms of a CEO. Yes, Phoenix was growing up.

With Phoenix in town, Daddy came to visit with a woman who, surprisingly, seemed to be his age or at least close. I could tell she had money when they showed up in her Lincoln LS, with her swinging a Chanel bag and wearing some unnamed designer outfit. A little flashy, but that's how he liked them. She was pleasant enough and even knew who Phoenix was. I watched her paw all over my father.

The atmosphere was just too relaxed for Phoenix to only be my boss, and Daddy immediately picked up on this. Daddy's hugging me and whispering in my ear, "I see you taking good care of yourself, Sasha," confirmed that he knew there was more to my relationship with Phoenix than just business. But Daddy was cool and didn't do anything to embarrass me. At Phoenix's request, I'd fixed a pot of homemade sauce and linguini, along with a salad and garlic bread. I even made cannolis for dessert. Daddy didn't say it, but I knew he liked it when I showed off my Italian cooking skills. Along with the wine I'd brought, I'd also made a pitcher of Long Island Iced Tea. The more Daddy and Phoenix drank, the more I worried that they would relax and say too much. As I feared, I overheard Daddy tell Phoenix, "I appreciate you taking care of my daughter." Before more could be said, I moved quickly to end dinner. I got Phoenix to take some pictures and sign some autographs, then I sent Daddy home.

That stay at my house was the first time Phoenix and I really allowed ourselves to show affection. We lay in bed, wrapped around each other, our long legs entwined like a Philly pretzel as we ate hot wings and watched movies.

During those two days Phoenix ravished me sexually. He found every nook and cranny inside my body, and occasionally I urged him to slow down and take his time with me. The road to the finish line was always more fun than the finish itself.

Before his visit was over, Phoenix had an unusual request. He wanted me to have a small vault installed inside my house. I knew he had one in each of his homes to store money, jewelry, and a few guns, but I thought it was strange that he was insisting I get one, too. I told him I had a security system linked to the police station, but that wasn't his reason. Phoenix wanted to hide a few things, and since I was interested in what they were, I agreed to having a small steel box hidden in the floor of my bedroom closet. In return for my silence he told me I could get a car that would totally belong to me. I immediately chose a silver BMW 735I to go along with my Lexus. Phoenix told me that every month a package would arrive via Federal Express, and I was to simply put it in the vault.

Now, I had been aware, mostly from eavesdropping, that Phoenix had been involved with a Chicago jeweler who'd been killed while on business in New York. The details of the man's death were hazy, but I knew that Phoenix, as well as a few other athletes, were questioned about their business relationships with the jeweler. I just hoped his putting a vault in my house didn't put me at risk. If it did, I hoped the risk would pay off.

Soon after Phoenix left Philly, Crystal called and said she needed to fly into town to speak with me. I wasn't concerned that she knew about Phoenix and me because she hinted that the visit was about Phoenix's birthday in two weeks. Mitchell had told me to build a solid relationship with Crystal but not to make her my friend, and I'd done just that.

I met Crystal one afternoon for lunch at Rouge on Rittenhouse Square. She was all excited and asked me to assist her in planning a birthday party for Phoenix at their home in Chicago. She rarely asked anything of me so I couldn't turn her down. And she was offering me $2,500 for my help.

I agreed and we made some preliminary plans. It was going to be a surprise party and Crystal was excited that we would have a secret Phoenix knew nothing about, since he always claimed to know everything. My role would be to secure the guests and handle the logistics and the entertainment.

For the next two weeks we planned his party. Spending so much time with her made me feel guilty about fucking her man. As the day of the party neared, Crystal insisted I meet her in Chicago so we could shop for clothes. So there we were, in and out of shops on Michigan Avenue buying dresses, shoes, bags, and accessories. As I watched Crystal, I hoped she would remain ignorant of my relationship with Phoenix.

Finally, the party day arrived, and the people who'd shown up on his behalf did surprise Phoenix. I'd invited Trent, but he was wrapped up preparing for a fund-raiser that was being held the following evening in New Jersey. I would be returning to New Jersey to accompany him.

Phoenix's party was supposed to be a classy affair, but I'd kept in mind that Phoenix Carter was a young boy. His hip-hop friends were there and took care of all the entertainment in addition to inviting some women, video girls mostly, to add to the ambience.

Since it was the end of the season and everybody wasn't in the playoffs, a lot of Phoenix's fellow athletes were in attendance: KG, Half-Man-Half-Amazing, AI, Starbury, and MJ, who I would've much rather been sleeping with. At Mitchell's suggestion, I'd also invited Phoenix's staff and business partners, which included folks from Nike, Pepsi, Gatorade, Timberland, American Express, and Mercedes.

The atmosphere was hot, the music loud, and you could find people throughout the house doing everything from dancing to making deals. The food was catered from a mix of Phoenix's favorite restaurants and Cristal and Moët flowed from a fountain all night. I couldn't imagine what gifts people would bring a millionaire, but they brought things that I knew Phoenix would never use or wear, things he'd probably just give away. Looking around at his guests and thinking of all my accomplishments, I realized I'd finally made the big league. And I knew my time was running out.

Phoenix treated me like his most prized employee during the party. Too often, though, I found him near me when I was talking to other men, and he sometimes abruptly interrupted our conversations while touching me a little too familiarly. He never said it, but I knew Phoenix didn't want another man near me. He'd accepted Trent because Trent didn't travel in his circle and he enjoyed knowing I had a man waiting for me in New Jersey while he was fucking me at every opportunity.

It was practically 4:00 A.M. when I realized that almost everyone had left. Only Phoenix's close friends remained. As I made my way to the guesthouse, Crystal stopped me.

"Sasha, can you come with me please?" she tentatively asked.

For a moment I panicked, thinking maybe she was about to confront me. Maybe Phoenix had spent too much time near me, and made Crystal suspicious.

"I wanted to give you a little something to say thank you," Crystal said, motioning for me to follow her into their bedroom.

I was nervous and hoped she couldn't tell. "Crystal, you paid me. That's enough."

"It's obvious, Sasha, that you've done more for Phoenix

than I can possibly imagine. We wanted to give you something to show our appreciation." At that moment Phoenix walked into the room. I could hear my heart pounding loudly as I awkwardly found myself standing between the two of them in their bedroom. Smiling, Phoenix put his arm around my shoulders and guided me to sit on the bed. I couldn't imagine what the hell they could give me. I just wanted to hurry up and get out from between them.

Crystal then opened her jewelry cabinet and pulled out an unwrapped, long, narrow, blue box which, surprisingly, held a 22-inch platinum necklace. Before I could find the words to thank her, she pulled out a second box, a smaller one. In it was a platinum and diamond watch pendant to be hung from the necklace. Even though the gift appeared costly, which was typical of Phoenix, both pieces were actually classy, not like some of the gaudy jewelry they wore.

I was speechless. Although I tried not to cry, tears fell down my face. Not because of the gift, but because of the backstabbing person I was. By now Crystal and Phoenix were standing so close to me I could barely breathe. I needed to get out of there. I kissed Crystal on the cheek and thanked her, all the while trying not to look at Phoenix. Before I could rush out of the room Phoenix hugged me, and the feel of his adulterous arms around me made me almost want to spit on him.

Finally, I made it to the guesthouse. I took a long shower and washed my hair. I was exhausted. There was no way I would continue with Phoenix. I wouldn't endure another season, no matter what the price.

Once I was in bed I phoned Trent to see how the race

Brenda L. Thomas

was going. He, too, sounded exhausted and made me promise I'd be at Newark Airport by noon tomorrow so we could spend some quality lovemaking time before the fund-raiser. I told him about the gift from Crystal and he said I deserved that and more. He didn't think Phoenix appreciated all I did for him. Trent's main complaint was that Phoenix was too needy of me.

After enjoying a little phone sex, we said good night and I drifted off to sleep. I was eager to get home to him.

It must have been about 6:00 A.M. when I heard a light tapping at my door. It could only be Phoenix.

"I know you hear me," he said as he turned the knob and entered the room.

I sat up in bed. "What are you doing here?"

"C'mon. I need you, Sasha." he answered, standing at the foot of the bed.

"This is the wrong fucking place to be needing me. Go to your damn wife."

"She ain't my fucking wife yet!" he said smugly. I could tell he was fucked up. He'd been smoking blunts and doing shots of Grand Marnier all night. As he moved closer to the bed, I wrapped the sheet around my naked body.

"Listen, just let me—"

"Let you what, Phoenix? Fuck me while Crystal is a few feet away?" I could see he was getting agitated; his face tightened. It was a look I'd seen on the court when he was desperate for the last shot.

He raised his voice, slurring his words. "What the fuck do you care? You ain't cared about Crystal before!"

"Well, I care about her now. You know what, Phoenix?

It's over and I don't just mean this shit we been doing. I'm quitting!"

He laughed. "Bitch, you ain't going nowhere. You just biting Crystal's ass 'cause she gave you that platinum and ice," he said nonchalantly, sitting on the bed and unbuckling his belt. I moved closer to the headboard and threatened to call Trey.

"Trey can't help you. He left with some bitch."

"Well, I'll call Crystal in her room then."

"Yeah, and what you gonna tell her? That you been fucking me and tonight you don't wanna give it up?"

He was right. What would I tell her? It was inconceivable to Phoenix that I didn't want to give myself to him. I tried to turn from him but he grabbed me by the throat, forcing my face close to his.

Gagging, I said, "Phoenix, please. I can't."

"Fuck that. Yes the fuck you can!"

I managed to loosen his grip and quickly got up from the bed. I tried to go into the bathroom but he stepped in front of me and held my arms. We tussled as I tried to get out of his grip, but, even fucked up, he was too strong for me. I fell against the dresser, knocking my toiletries over and onto the floor. He wrestled me to the floor, all the while telling me how good I was to him. I screamed at him as I fought to get loose. He slapped me and I stilled. I tasted blood.

"Don't make me do this, Sasha. Please."

In an effort to fight him off, I grabbed for his platinum chain, scratching him on the neck. He tried to pull my hand loose, but I yanked even harder until his chain snapped. But that didn't stop him.

I cried, "Phoenix, please stop. I can't do this anymore."

Suddenly he picked me up and threw me on the bed.

"You know I need this, Sasha. Right? I only do it because I love you," he said, pinning me to the bed with his knee across my stomach. I winced from the pain but he wouldn't relent.

He removed his pants and boxers all at once, still holding me with one hand. I lay there limp beneath him trying to figure out a way to convince him to leave. Straddling me, he roughly pushed a finger inside me while whispering in my ear.

"Don't you know how fucking bad I wanted you tonight? Why you making me do this shit? Shit, I fucking love your ass. Feel how hard you got my dick."

I didn't respond, just lay there crying. He slid down my body and buried his head between my legs licking me until I could feel my body defy me. As my orgasm melted around his tongue, I asked myself why was this happening? Why couldn't I control my own body? After Phoenix had tasted his fill, he rose up on his knees, put both of my legs across one of his shoulders, and plunged himself deep into me. He came almost instantly.

Phoenix knew he'd made me come. To prove his power over me he pushed his finger into me, then put it to my lips and grinned. I looked in his eyes. I wanted to tell him I hated him but knew it wouldn't matter. Finished with me, he picked his broken platinum chain off the floor, stuffed it in his pocket, and walked out. I realized that my affair with Phoenix had sucked the life out of me. He had no remorse.

After he left I just lay there trembling under the covers. I began to cry, thinking maybe I really did belong to him. I hated myself for what I had become. I phoned

Arshell and tried to tell her what happened. She couldn't talk with Wayne lying next to her in bed but said we'd talk later when we got to Trent's fund-raiser.

After I hung up the phone I gathered the strength to pull myself together. I mean, maybe this episode with Phoenix wasn't that bad. Wasn't it just a piece of pussy? I had to leave for the airport in a few hours, so I staggered to the shower then got dressed.

Once I was ready I phoned Trey's room, as he was supposed to be taking me to the airport. When he came to get my bags and saw my swollen lip, he asked me if I was okay. I told him I hoped the swelling would disappear before I reached New Jersey. I knew I didn't have to explain more. He knew Phoenix was the cause. I went to the Benz to wait for him. He showed up with a plastic bag filled with ice.

As I sat in first class I realized that I'd have to act as if nothing happened when I saw Trent. I longed for one of those nights when Trent and I would spend the evening together without talking. After what had just happened with Phoenix, I wasn't sure I could go back to Trent with so much guilt weighing me down. To bolster my courage I asked the airline attendant for a double shot of Remy Martin. By the time I reached Newark Airport I was half drunk.

Trent's arms consumed me the moment I walked off the plane. All I could do was cry. He laughed. He thought I was crying because I missed him. We hadn't seen each other in almost a month. But my tears were so much more. I was crying because I'd again fucked up my life and was scared of how all this would end. Would someone die again because of my fucked-up choices? Of course this was no time to figure it all out. I pushed my worries into the back of my mind and told myself it was one of the hazards of the job. I told Trent I missed him and was glad to be home.

As we traveled to his condo, making love was the last thing I wanted to do. But I knew I couldn't turn him down. I couldn't let on that anything was wrong. Why did he have to be so damn happy to see me? The swelling in my lip had gone down, but when I finally removed my sunglasses, Trent questioned my puffy eyes. I played it off, saying that I hadn't slept in two days. That's when he suggested that I needed a real vacation.

Poor Trent had no idea what I really needed and neither did I.

Eventually, we wound up in bed. I lay there responding to Trent as if he were all that mattered. I said all the things I knew he wanted to hear. It was the first time I ever faked it with him.

"Oh, Trent. I love you," I whispered against his neck. But did I?

"Trent, it feels so good to be back home." How could it, when my body still ached from Phoenix's violent love-making?

"I missed you. Oh, I missed you so much." I thought about all the men I'd repeated those words to and wondered if I'd ever meant them.

I got through the rest of the afternoon by falling asleep. Hours later, Trent woke me up to get dressed for the fund-raiser. While Trent was in the shower I checked the messages on my cell phone. Six calls were from Phoenix, begging for forgiveness. What he was really begging for was my silence. In each of his messages he asked me what it would take for him to keep me.

As I was pinning my hair up, I heard Trent in the living room arguing with someone about the union. I was stunned when Trent threatened to kill somebody. He sounded like a madman. Was everybody going crazy?

After I heard Trent's visitor leave, I went downstairs and asked him what was wrong.

"Sasha, stay outta this, alright?"

Even though he didn't want to talk about it, I asked him about pieces of the conversation I'd heard. Instead of answering he turned, looked at me with a seriousness that made me cringe and walked away. It was now obvious that running for IBEW president wasn't going to be an easy feat for a brother.

I'd convinced Trent to rent a limo for the night so Wayne and Arshell could ride with us. When they arrived at the condo I couldn't even meet Arshell's eyes. There would obviously be no time for Arshell and me to talk before leaving for the Sheraton in East Rutherford.

As Trent and I made our way through the mirrored lobby, I looked at us, the happy couple. Trent was wearing a black double-breasted Versace suit and the black Ferragamo shoes I'd forced him to buy. He looked good. How could I not be proud to be his woman? I smiled as we entered the crowded ballroom and greeted people. I could tell Trent was happy to have me beside him because he couldn't stop telling me how beautiful I was. I wore a charcoal-colored Dolce & Gabbana dress that was cut down in the back so deep you could just about see the crack of my ass. With that I wore a pair of Jimmy Choo heels I'd special ordered through one of Phoenix's contacts. I also wore the tennis bracelet I'd gotten from Phoenix and a pair of diamond hoops.

After about an hour of mingling, Trent's campaign manager silenced the crowd to make a few announcements. To my astonishment, as Trent's campaign manager was reading off the list of donations, I heard her say Phoenix Carter, $5,000, which received loud applause from the audience, and some people, knowing I worked for Phoenix, turned and smiled at me. I couldn't believe Phoenix. He'd forced himself on me earlier that morning and now he was contributing to Trent's campaign, probably just to let me know how much power he had.

While Trent mingled with his guests, Arshell and I went into the lobby to talk. I told her what happened with Phoenix and quickly admitted that it was my fault for having been with him in the first place. Arshell felt otherwise. She tried to convince me that Phoenix had raped me both physically and spiritually.

"Sasha, do you know what rape is? It's not about sex with Phoenix. It's about power and control. You're clinging to a situation that has outlived its usefulness. He's made you compromise all your morals and values."

I was trying not to cry as she talked.

"I mean . . . look, Sasha. You can be a whore, who gives a fuck? Sometimes I wish I could fuck a few different men, but damn, don't let Phoenix control your life. Do you really wanna lose Trent over that nigga?"

Maybe I did. I didn't deserve a man like Trent.

I could barely speak up. "Arshell, I'm bought and paid for. Look at it. Ever since Cole—"

"Shut up with that Cole shit. You can't ruin your life because his crazy-ass wife killed herself. How long are you going to blame yourself? What happened to the person you used to be? When's the last time you read a book? Lit a candle? Hell, all the plants at your house are dead! Phoenix was never there for you. What he provided was just an illusion."

I tried to remain calm, but the truth of Arshell's words made me start crying. That's when Wayne R. Wayne walked up to us.

"What's wrong with Sasha?" he asked. Instead of answering, I ran to the ladies' room.

It was well past midnight when the four of us returned in the limo to Trent's condo. After Arshell and Wayne left, I did something that I only did with Phoenix—I pulled a joint out of my purse and lit it. The sweet smell of it made me begin to relax. Trent and I sat quietly on the living room sofa, passing the joint back and forth.

"Sasha, we need to start thinking about our future. What do you think about us getting married?" he asked, as he ran his hand down the back of my dress to touch my ass.

"Yo, are you serious?" I caught myself. I was starting to sound like Phoenix and his thug friends and it wasn't the first time. I looked at Trent, who hadn't even noticed. I passed him the joint.

"I wouldn't want to marry anybody but you," I said, a smile in my voice. Trent smiled in response. "But now I have something to say."

"What?"

"I'm quitting my job with Phoenix."

"When? I mean why?" he asked, putting the joint out in the ashtray.

"It's just time to move on."

"Is that all there is?"

Did he expect there to be more?

"Yes. If I'm going to be your first lady, I need to be closer to my husband."

"Well, you need to be sure that's what you really want, 'cause you've been real important to Phoenix."

Was he saying this because Phoenix had just given him $5,000? Was he now ready to reap some of the benefits of my fucking Phoenix? I didn't answer, just moved to the coffee table in front of the sofa and slid my dress up to my thighs.

"Why don't you stop worrying about Phoenix and take care of your wife?"

Since the incident in Chicago, Phoenix repeatedly tried to tell me he was sorry, but I kept all our meetings and phone conversations strictly business. I'd even threatened to press charges if he ever tried to touch me again. He tried to buy me back into his graces with all the things he thought I wanted. But all I really wanted was to be free of him. First, I declined all his presents—an all expenses paid trip to Tahiti for Trent and me and a 500SL Mercedes-Benz. In one voice mail he even said he'd leave Crystal. I declined everything, and never responded to his talk of leaving Crystal.

But I knew I was weakening.

One morning while Phoenix and I sat in a conference room at Sony waiting to discuss an endorsement deal, he gently slid a box toward me. I knew he was trying to win me back with jewelry. My heart began beating rapidly. I couldn't resist—his eyes begged me to open it. I lifted the hinge that held it closed and looked at the pair of four-carat diamond earrings that I'd been waiting for since the first time I'd slept with him. These were bigger than Crystal's. I just shook my head. Without looking, I could feel him relax, realizing that he'd finally won me back. Before I could thank him, the Sony execs walked into the room.

Phoenix patted my thigh under the table and whispered, "Yeah, now I got my Sasha back."

By now I was so torn with what and who I wanted that I could barely stay focused. Was I actually so materialistic that I could be bought with diamonds? I knew now that Phoenix had me hooked and I had to find a way to rid myself of him if I was ever going to be Trent's wife.

The effect of my sordid relationship with Phoenix began to bring out an ugly side of me. My emotions were spiraling out of control. I was short-tempered with Trent and I began to avoid him. I wasn't even returning Arshell's phone calls. I knew I was out of hand when I found myself arguing with Phoenix. Instead of us returning to our usual shit, he began to play games with me. After the gift, he'd tease me but wouldn't sleep with me. I found myself wanting him, craving him. I tried to tell myself that I didn't care, yet I was disappointed when he didn't want me. And I found myself wanting him even more.

Trent had won the election and wanted to look for an engagement ring, but I kept making excuses. My son also wanted to know why I was dragging my feet about the engagement. I guess he wanted to see me settled with someone so that he wouldn't have to worry about his mother.

Oddly, I found myself getting jealous of Crystal, who had finally set a date for her wedding to Phoenix. I mean, it was hard to sit by and watch her spend money and make plans for their big day when I couldn't even look Trent in the eye.

During all this time, I'd been collecting the FedEx packages Phoenix sent to my house. Curious about what was inside those FedEx packages, I opened one and discovered it contained diamonds wrapped in black felt. I immediately wished I hadn't looked because I had the feeling that Phoenix was getting himself into real trouble. Why else would he be hiding diamonds in my house?

Even though his wedding was around the corner, Phoenix never stopped his sexual games. Phoenix finally gave me what I'd been craving one particular night when I was in Chicago while he was in the finals of the playoffs. He didn't know I was in town until I called his cell phone late that night. Before I knew it, he was knocking on my hotel door. After hesitating, I opened the door and there he stood—a six-foot-nine thug in a gray Sean John sweatsuit that hung from his body with attitude. Who was I fooling? I wanted this man.

He entered the room and strolled over to me with a look of ownership. He asked me why I hadn't told him I was in Chicago and why I hadn't come to the game. I tried to explain that I'd arrived late and was tired, especially since we had to attend a meeting with the team owners in the morning. He accused me of lying because Crystal had said she'd talked to me earlier in the day and had asked me to go with her to see her wedding gown.

I hated thinking about his wedding, so I cut him off. "I don't want to hear about Crystal, her fucking Vera Wang dress, or none of that bullshit!"

"Oh, so that's why you won't help her with the wedding," Phoenix exclaimed. "Wait a minute—I know you ain't jealous. You kidding, right?"

I screamed at him, knowing all of this was leading

nowhere. "Fuck no. I ain't jealous, I'm getting married, too! I'm just tired of fucking with you."

He didn't say anything, just sat slouched down in a chair by the bed.

"What do you mean fucking with you? I haven't touched you, Sasha."

"Look, Phoenix, you're getting married, and I'm engaged to Trent, so please let's stop this bullshit."

Instead of responding, he began quoting some damn rap song by Philly's Most Wanted—*"excuse me chick, what's your name? 'coupla dollas ain't it. So wuz your game?"*—as if I didn't understand what it meant. I hated him.

"Sasha," he said calmly, as he reached for me. "I don't care if both of us get married. I'm still gonna fuck you."

Why was I relieved? He was so damn sure of himself as he reached his hand between my legs, grabbing a handful of pussy.

"Look, I know we fucked up doing this shit too much, but it's too late now. I'm never letting you go."

I grabbed him by that platinum cross, pulled his mouth to mine, and kissed him. He pulled away and said, "Yeah, right. That's what I thought you wanted."

13

PROTECTOR OF MEN

June 2001

There were some decisions I had to make, and the only way to clear my head was to visit Arshell. I had been ignoring her for too long, and of all the things I'd sacrificed, I wouldn't risk losing her.

I flew from Chicago to BWI to spend the day with her. Arshell picked me up, and we drove to her house so we could talk. Actually, it was more so I could listen. She put it real simple. Resign from my position with Phoenix, get honest with Trent (not about everything), and go into therapy. It seemed Trent had even phoned her to find out why I was being so hesitant about moving forward with our wedding plans. It was the first time I was caught speechless. I could no longer rationalize or justify my actions.

After my visit with Arshell, I hired a limo to drive me home to Philly. To my surprise, on my home voice mail was a message from Owen telling me that his wife was expecting. I called to congratulate him, but he sensed how hard it was for me to share in his happiness.

"Mom, is something wrong?" he asked.

"No, I'm OK," I mumbled.

"Well, that means something's wrong. Have you heard from Cole?" he always thought any problem I had was related to Cole, probably because he knew how much I'd loved him.

"Oh, Owen, I wish it was that simple. But nothing in my life is simple, not relationships, not work. I just want—"

"What's wrong with work?"

I remained silent as I figured out how to answer Owen's question.

"Mom, is something going on with you and Phoenix?" he asked impatiently.

I couldn't answer him because I didn't want to lie.

"Mom, Mom, please tell me you're not fucking that boy!"

"Owen, it's not what you think. It's not the same as Cole. It just happened."

"Mom, nothing just happens with you!"

"Oh, please just let me explain."

"No, Ma. I gotta go." And he hung up.

Owen had never done that before. Even with all the wrong decisions I'd made and warnings he'd given me, he'd never just hung up and shut me out of his life. Was I now gonna lose him too? Rather than call back, I decided to wait until I had better control of my situation. Then I'd go talk to him in person.

I wanted to keep my leaving Phoenix as simple and professional as possible, so I phoned Mitchell and requested a meeting the following day. In his office I simply told him the situation—my sleeping with Phoenix, the rape, and all the gifts. I told him I thought our relationship was out of control.

Mitchell didn't respond at first, just stood up and walked around his office, staring at me from across the room. He then sat on the couch and motioned for me to sit next to him.

"What happened, Sasha? I mean, how did you let it happen? You're supposed to be older, mature. That's why I thought you could handle him."

"Well, I couldn't," I said, determined not to cry.

"What do you want to do?" he asked, sounding defeated.

I handed him the resignation letter. After reading it, he shook his head in disbelief.

"You know he's not gonna *let* you quit."

"What do you mean, *let* me?"

"He'll offer you more money. Sasha, he really likes you. You're so good for him."

"Mitchell, are you asking me to stay, to keep fucking this man?" I got up and paced the room.

"Well . . . I mean, you could stop and just tell him it has to be strictly professional."

"Mitchell, it's too late for that. Obviously you don't know your boy very well. Every time he sees me he wants to fuck. He doesn't care who's around or where we are. He thinks he fucking owns me. And you know what's even more fucked up? I'm starting to believe he does. But the difference is I don't wanna be part of his entourage anymore." I paused. "Mitchell, please talk to him."

"Sasha, who is gonna do your job?" he asked.

"I don't know. Maybe one of his other women. One of the secretaries at his company would be glad to take my job. Anyway, that's not my problem."

"So, what do you want? You know there's going to be some legal ramifications."

I started walking toward the door. "Look, just give him the letter and get back to me."

"When was the last time you spoke to him?" he asked.

"Well, we haven't really talked in about a week. We've just been leaving each other voice mails."

"Alright. Let me try to talk to him."

Later that night, Mitchell called me on my cell while I was at Trent's. I took the phone into the kitchen.

"Sasha, look. It's not good," Mitchell said, sounding like he was afraid to tell me about Phoenix's reaction.

"I'm listening."

"Like I predicted, Phoenix refuses to let you go. He says he'll do whatever you want. He'll give you more money, a new house, car. He says he can't live without you, that you owe him."

"I owe him! Is he fucking crazy? I made Phoenix fucking Carter the man he is off the court and he says I owe him!"

"He wants you to fly to Chicago and talk to him. Maybe you should try talking with him. He says that he'll stop having sex with you but he needs you by his side."

"Fuck that, Mitchell! I'm not for sale anymore!"

"Well, I might as well tell you that he says he'll make sure you don't work for any other celebrities. He can blackball you, Sasha."

I didn't realize I was screaming. "You know what, Mitchell? If Phoenix fucks with me, I'll ruin his goddamn career. I'll let Crystal know we've been fucking and, if I have to, I'll go to the press and tell them all the other corrupt shit that's been going on throughout the league and Carter Enterprises. Do you think I don't know what's in them damn FedEx envelopes, Mitchell? You think I'm gonna keep my mouth shut about that if he fucks with me?"

As soon as the words were out of my mouth I regretted it. I turned, there stood Trent, and from the look on his face I knew he'd heard every word I'd said, especially about me fucking Phoenix. We stood staring at each other. I could hear Mitchell talking but I wasn't listening. Trent walked away and I told Mitchell, who was in midsentence, that I'd have to call him back. I slowly walked into the living room.

"Trent, please just listen to me," I pleaded.

"You dirty bitch! I knew there was more to you and him than just fucking work!"

"Please, Trent. You don't understand."

"Fuck no. Get the fuck out!"

I went to him. "Please, Trent, let me at least explain! I—"

He didn't let me finish, just unleashed his anger by backhanding me across the face.

I knew then there was no more to be said. Anyway, what could I have said? Sorry would have meant nothing. Explanations would've been useless, but somehow I wanted to explain. Wanted to finally tell him about Cole and about how Phoenix had pulled me into his life and that the sex was only because I'd been weak, been empty. That it was him I really loved. But that would've all been bullshit.

Trent's hardened face warned me not to say anything, so I just picked up my bag from the recliner and walked out. As I opened the door, I looked back to see if maybe I could say something. But Trent turned his head, reached for the television remote, and acted as if I'd already gone.

14

THE NIGHTMARE

July 2001

*F*irst I was him and then I was her. The sex was so strong. I
found myself lying underneath her with all her weight on me,
talking to me. The lovemaking was good, long-awaited. It was as
if she had the dick and was pushing it deeper and deeper inside of
me. My body, though, was rising to meet her and the thrusts
against me. Why was it so good? I couldn't stop the thoughts or the
act I was caught up in. Didn't she realize who I was? Regardless
that it had been years since she'd seen me. Hadn't been around me
growing up, didn't know if I'd needed training wheels to ride a bike
or if I played with snakes. All we both seemed to know is that we
wanted each other.

And then I was her. Giving it to him, making him love it
and me. I knew it was good for him. I could tell by the way he

cried out "Oh, Mommy. I missed you." But he hadn't asked me to stop and I wouldn't have been able to. It wasn't that he looked like his father; it was just that I longed to be his mother, his mommy. He was hurting, and loving him was the only way I knew how to heal that pain.

I woke up sweating, my pussy throbbing as if I had stopped myself short of coming. I still had to be dreaming but, no, the sun was coming through my blinds. I quickly closed my legs. Damn, why were my thighs wet? My pussy needed me, a finger, a stroke, anything to make the throbbing and yearning go away. But I was scared, so I squeezed my legs tighter and rolled over to figure out what had gone wrong in my mind during the night. Why had I dreamed about a mother and son having sex and why had I been both of them?

After having this nightmare I knew it was time to talk to somebody about what had happened in my life. It was time to go beneath the surface of my false strength and bravery. I finally followed Arshell's suggestion. I made an appointment with a psychologist.

While waiting to hear from Mitchell over the next two weeks, I focused my attention on finding another job. I realized it would be hard to find a position that would pay $150K plus expenses, in addition to the perks I received from being with Phoenix. I didn't even know what kind of job I was looking for. But what I did know was that corporate America would give me something stable, no traveling, just nine-to-five and two weeks vacation in the summer. I needed to reestablish myself through honest work that had a purpose.

The position I now found myself in was much different than anything I'd ever dreamed for myself. I mean, my idea of a successful career as a young girl was whatever career the latest Barbie doll had, whether it be airline stewardess or nurse.

I had no idea what I wanted to be when I grew up, I just grew up. Once I graduated high school, I tried college for a year at Temple but it moved too slow, so I got a job at Blue Cross. That's where I met Owen's father. After we married, I moved on to become an executive secretary at Wharton. Once the marriage was over, I began working for Mitchell & Ness and all my troubles began.

Now here I was, starting all over again. I had a professional résumé done and I was registered with a headhunter. Where could I go? Where could I hide? I searched D.C., L.A., Atlanta, and Boston. Everything seemed boring to me. I couldn't imagine myself returning to the standard secretarial life. Sitting in an office all day taking orders, typing memos, curbing personal calls, and scheduling meetings would drive me crazy. And, of course, there were the one-hour lunches spent with white girls sharing personal stories, women who otherwise wouldn't speak to me. I didn't know what I'd do but I couldn't return to that, at least not right away.

My bills were all current and, thanks to Phoenix, my house was paid off. I'd saved $100K in cash, made wise investments in the past few years, so at least I could afford to take some time off. I knew I'd probably walk away with a tidy sum of money.

As I walked the streets of Chestnut Hill, nothing seemed familiar. My neighbors' faces had even changed. There were new families, mostly young professional couples, who knew nothing about Sasha Borianni. I was glad for the strangers, yet missed the familiarity. Even though I tried to absorb myself in the job search, many days and nights I found myself doing what most women do when they're hurting. I'd thrown away any Xanax I'd had left over, so all I could do was drink wine. Some nights I'd go through two bottles. WDAS FM once again became a comfort to me, as Luther Vandross's words spelled out my pain, reminding me *"That hearts get broken all the time."* What was even more true was that this time *"I'd broken mine and become one of love's casualties."* It's funny how music can hurt you and heal you at the same time. I attempted to turn away from the music that was speaking my pain but I was curious to find out who the hell this chick Jill Scott was that everyone in Philly kept playing. Had I really been out of touch that long? It was this sister's words that made me realize that my life was no longer defined by one of Phoenix's rap songs. My relationship with Trent had been a ballad set to her tune of "Taking a Long Walk" but because of my selfishness, I was clearly *"swimming upstream,"* most likely to the unknown.

Daddy phoned, but I wouldn't take his calls. I assumed Owen had told him what happened. Finally, he left a message saying, "Sasha, like I've always told you, life is like a crap game. If you don't win on the first roll, you just shoot the damn dice again. Remember, baby, Daddy loves you. Call me, alright?"

With the NBA season over and Chicago having won the championship, Phoenix would now be all that he'd imagined himself to be. He just wouldn't have me along for the ride.

Mitchell eventually calmed Phoenix down and proceeded to draw up legal documents for my exit from

Carter Enterprises. I was due a large severance package. According to my contract, I would be paid for the remainder of the year and the bonus money Phoenix owed me, totaling $275K. I knew some of that was hush money. Unfortunately, I would have to return the Lexus and BMW. I'd hardly driven the cars. They were usually either parked at my house or Trent's. The first stipulation was that I work to train his new assistant, and any files at my home were to be turned over to Mitchell. And, of course, I had to sign a confidentiality agreement, and there was to be no publicity. The last stipulation was that I meet with Phoenix.

We agreed to meet at Mitchell's office, and for the first time in a long time I didn't care what I wore. When I got there, Phoenix had already arrived. Mitchell directed me to the conference room and told me to holler if I needed him. I was feeling confident until I walked into the room and saw Phoenix spin around in that chair. He rarely wore suits, but today he had on a chocolate-brown, Hugo Boss, single-breasted linen suit that I'd picked out. Underneath he had on a cream-colored mock turtleneck by Ermenegildo Zegna and a pair of chocolate-brown Prada shoes. His bald head was shining, as were the diamond hoops in both his ears. I wasn't sure if I preferred him as a boy or a man.

He stood up and walked toward me, and I realized how truly weak I was for him. He grabbed me around the shoulders with one arm and quickly kissed me on the mouth, tracing my lips with his tongue.

"Yo, what's up, Sasha?" he said, as I backed away from him.

I didn't answer, just took a seat. I expected him to sit

across from me or maybe at the head of the conference table, but, no, he sat right next to me. I could smell the Angel cologne he was wearing and felt myself begin to want him. Then he sat back, slouched down in his chair, resting one hand on his Gucci belt. He smiled that sly grin at me.

Nervously, I stood up. "Look, Phoenix. I can't work for you anymore." I stammered.

"Why not?" he asked, not even looking at me.

"You know why not," I said, hoping I did.

"Maybe I do, maybe I don't. How 'bout you need to tell me." He said this casually, but he looked at me intently, as if he dared me to find a reason not to want him.

"Look, I can't be your business manager and your ho, okay?"

"Damn. Who said you was all that?" he asked, stroking himself, for my benefit, I'm sure.

"Phoenix, I don't know why we had to meet anyway. It's pretty cut-and-dry. I'm resigning," I said, standing behind the chair I'd been sitting in.

"Do you think you can just up and go, just like that? What about how I feel?" He sounded almost pathetic.

"That's not my problem," I said, as I sat back down, this time farther away from him. "And, by the way, you might wanna get your damn diamonds out of that vault at my house," I added, trying to change the subject. He looked surprised that I knew what was inside the packages.

"I'll send somebody for it. Look, let me ask you something. You think you gonna be satisfied with that fucking Trent nigga? C'mon, you and I both know you need more than that, Sasha."

I ignored him. I wasn't about to tell him that, because of him, I'd already lost Trent. "Don't fucking patronize me, you bastard!"

He got up and moved toward me. I stood my ground. I thought he would grab me and I almost wanted him to. Instead, he just stood towering over me. He didn't speak, he just stared down at me until I could feel my panties get wet, like they did the first time I met him. To gain some leverage I stood up.

"Alright, fuck it. If that's what you want!" he said, moving close to me. I shook my head yes and tried to walk around him, but this time he grabbed me from behind, cupped one of my breasts, and whispered in my ear, his tongue touching my lobe, "So you don't wanna fuck me anymore?"

Then it clicked. He was about to lose all his power and control over me. I turned around, grabbed him by the dick, and said, "Fuck no."

15

SURRENDER

August 2001

I still hadn't heard from Trent and was scared to call him. He was now IBEW's president, and I'd recently seen him on the news holding his son. I wondered if he was with Paige, if they were a family. I hated the thought of it but knew I had no recourse considering the humiliation I'd caused him. But I was glad that he was doing well and only wished him the best. Later that night as I lay in bed unable to sleep, I decided to write him.

Dear Trent:

> *I pray for your understanding as you read this letter. I know there is no forgiving me for how I betrayed you. I guess writing you helps me see the real crime I've committed against*

you and the trust you put in me. Some days I just can't seem to sort it all out. I know there is no way to justify what I've done to you but there are some things I want to share.

Before I met you I'd been in love with a married man. I stayed in that relationship for five years, until one night Cole's wife broke in to my house. She shot herself in my bedroom doorway as I lay in bed with her husband.

Four months later I was working for Phoenix. Working for him in such a fast-paced environment seemed to fill in the spaces of my life that had previously been filled with ghosts. What I didn't realize was that attaching myself to someone of his stature made me vulnerable. He took advantage of that. What's worse, I let him. I felt worthless, but what did it matter? I'd held myself responsible for Paulette's death, which only compounded the guilt I'd always felt and hid of my mother having died giving birth to me. Now I was responsible for two deaths.

Ever since I was a child I'd hated the sight of blood, maybe because my father had told me that my mother had hemorrhaged so badly that I'd almost drowned in her blood as I was passing through the birth canal. And then there was Paulette's blood. It had soaked through my hardwood floors and it, too, drowned me. Although Owen cleaned it up, it took my very breath away, and months later I found myself still trying to scrub away the smell of death. And then one night, unable to sleep, I began rearranging my bedroom. Hidden under the bed, I found an earring, a gold hoop. At first I thought it was mine, until I reached for it and realized it was attached to skin crusted with blood. It had to have been Paulette's.

That night, without packing a bag, I ran out of the house and drove to D.C. where Phoenix had flown in for a game. I stayed with him that night, and he held me and tried to comfort me in his young arms. A year later those same arms were reaching out to me for other reasons, and somehow I felt obligated.

Then I met you. You were the first man to enter my home since Cole. What's more, you were the first to sleep in my bed. Trent, you had the ability to quell the ghosts. Your presence enabled me to sleep through the night, something I hadn't done since the tragedy.

But none of this is an excuse for how I deceived you, for the pain I caused. I love you, Trent, but I was scared. Scared to let go of the security that Phoenix provided because, by then, I was trapped in a web of greed and a false allegiance.

Trent, I wanted so badly to be your wife. To be able to wipe my slate clean. To be a good woman and not live such a twisted life, but all that was taken away from me by my own hands. I have nobody to blame but myself.

I hope I haven't spoiled it for you, hope I haven't made it impossible for you to trust and love a woman again. You gave so much to me. That's why I left Phoenix—because I knew that you could provide me with a true reality. But it was too late. I should've known that my secrets wouldn't stay hidden forever.

Having been with Phoenix cost me a lot. Not only have I lost my values, but my sordid life has cost me you. It's not hard to understand or accept why I'll never hear from you again. I don't deserve a man like you. I just pray that one day your heart will soften in the places I've made hard. I broke the promise of my name, to be a protector of men, because I couldn't protect the one man who truly loved me.

I love you, Trent. Please take care of yourself and your heart and may you be blessed with a woman who truly deserves you.

Love always,
Sasha

EPILOGUE

I'd been in St. Lucia for two weeks. As I lay on the beach waiting for Arshell to spend a week with me, I thought back over the past few years. What had I really learned from all this? And more important, what behavior should I not repeat? Hell, I'd made a lot of mistakes. But hadn't I paid for them?

A sudden sadness filled me as I realized what it meant to be alone. No Trent, no Phoenix, and no Cole. I knew Trent would never take me back, but he did leave me a voice mail thanking me for the letter. Cole and I had finally closed the door on our relationship. We knew it would never pan out because of our troubled past. And Phoenix? Well, I prayed that I would never allow another man to hold me sexually hostage. Just today I'd seen him on the cover of *Fortune* magazine for an article on young millionaires. All I could do was look at his lips. Damn, why did memories always just pop into your mind whenever they felt like it? I lingered, looking at the photo for only for a few moments. I thought about my time with Phoenix. It wasn't a love affair we'd had. Just lust, just my need to please a man. For him, an ability to demand pleasure as often and from whomever he pleased. I just hoped there was some way I could salvage what was left of my emotions.

Going to therapy did seem to be helping. It was my therapist who'd suggested I take a vacation. During our sessions, she had assured me that we'd get to the core of the reasons why I seemed to have a ravenous sexual appetite and why I was so emotionally needy. For me the two went together.

There was also the issue of losing my mother. I had to face the insecurities that came from my having grown up without her. Her absence kept me from developing some of life's relationship skills, ones that mothers were able to pass on to their daughters.

I had no idea what I'd do once I returned to Philly, but I knew I'd be starting from scratch. Hell, I didn't even know if I'd stay in Philly. There were too many memories of too many men. But those memories didn't distract me from the fact that I hadn't had sex in about three months. There was no denying that I was starving for the touch of a man. I had been tempted by a few of the men I'd seen in St. Lucia but was trying to control myself by learning how to masturbate. But it was giving me no relief. As I lay there on the beach tanning, I realized that the fine-ass man lying across from me and smiling that familiar smile, was clearly with his wife. As I turned to lie on my stomach so he could have another view of me, I prayed that Arshell would hurry the hell up and arrive.